I0522703

THE CHAIN

R. J DYSON

absolutelyunprofessional.com

Wadsworth, OH

First Printing: 2022
ISBN 978-0-9997832-8-3
Absolutely Unprofessional
Wadsworth, OH 44281
absounpro.com
rjdysonsblog.com

for students who sense the glow in a
world sprinting through the dark

1 Chih-Ming

"**Y**ou look rough, Hesch," said Chih-ming, a fellow Observer from his dorm. "You sick or something?"

Heschel's cheeks glowed red. His eyes were a bit watery. "No. I'm fine, Ming. The wind is brutally cold today. Besides, I just left the infirmary for a routine check-up. They say I'm healthy enough to dominate the Deplorables."

"Oh yeah? I guess that's why you're a WAFE. They just tell me to stick to the approved regimen," said Chih-ming, looking away with a ruffled brow. Heschel couldn't tell if he was disappointed or disinterested in the lack of affirmation from the leadership. Chih was amiable but on the quieter side. A brilliant student, sure, but a bit of a gray cloud compared to the vibrant personality of Charlie. The Anti-Libertas had eliminated words like melancholy and depression. Instead, they trained gray clouds like Chih to consider themselves privileged to be central cogs in the Anti-Libertas machine.

"Listen, Chih, they tell all the Wide Awakes what they tell me. You know, to keep us on our toes. You know what's strange? I don't remember earning the blue belt. Not sure I'm really qualified for the Fully Empowered designation as an Observer." Heschel went to pat Chih-ming's shoulder but caught himself halfway, faking a wide stretch instead. He wasn't sure why he reached out to touch his friend. Touching wasn't allowed. Still, it seemed a natural response to a fellow Observer.

They were standing outside the entrance to their first session when Chih-ming paused. Young Observers flooding into the room parted around him like a stone in a river. Hesch stood behind him, patiently waiting.

"Hesch, can I ask you something?" said Chih-ming in a hoarse whisper.

"Yeah, I suppose. And I'm sure that whisper's not gonna attract any attention right here in the middle of the doorway."

"Was that sarcasm?" Chih-ming had secretly read about this ancient form of communication, though he hadn't actually participated in it. "So you just say the opposite of what's true. Wouldn't that qualify as a lie? Or is it what they used to call humor? In which case you *do* think it's a bad idea to have a private conversation right here."

Heschel smiled, not realizing that he was being snarky. "Chih, what's on your mind? We can wait until after the session if you want. Take a walk or something—it's up to you."

"Well, you've been going to the infirmary a lot lately, you know, since the fall Sojourn. And…well…"

Heschel's eyes grew wide. His cheeks turned a deep cherry red, and his back stiffened. "Come over here, Ming," he said, grabbing the young Observer's elbow and pulling him out of the doorway and into the hall.

Chih-ming began to panic. His shoulders slumped, and his words trailed off into a mumble.

"What else have you noticed, Ming? Don't hold back. Something's up. You and I didn't connect before the Sojourn, we worked on projects together, sure, but we didn't spend time together until after my long stint in the re-edu…I mean…in the infirmary with Joanna. Are you keeping tabs on me too?"

"I…I…I didn't mean it like that, Heschel. I…I just thought that, well, you see, Charlie…." Chih-ming stopped mid-sentence. His body froze like he'd just been caught by monitors for illegally sneaking extra rations. It was clear he had struck a nerve.

"Charlie, what? Who's Charlie, Ming? Why is that name familiar?" Heschel was still holding onto Chih-ming's elbow, squeezing tighter and tighter when the session buzzer sounded. "Relax, Chih. I'm sorry. I'm fine, really. Let's talk after your lunch. Maybe Joanna can help make sense of your ramblings."

Heschel scurried into the room with Chih-ming tailing closely behind. His mind hadn't been right these past few months since that long stint in The Adavis Center for Progress the previous fall. Like an endlessly dense fog, he was unable to grab ahold of a clear thought for any length of time. But there was something else. He couldn't quite remember that particular Sojourn. Neither could Joanna. Of course, images would flash through his mind now and again. Memories of events he didn't remember partaking in and people he didn't recognize—like Charlie—but it all seemed irrational and illegal. He would never sneak out of his flat at night, climb down cliffs, or search for hidden artifacts. After all, he was a Fully Empowered Wide Awake Observer—a model student at Compound 40.

2 Something Very Familiar

"Hey, what's up? You look pretty rough today, Hesch," said Joanna as he sat beside her. "Everything alright?"

"Sheesh! Do I look *that* bad?" he muttered.

"I take it I'm not the first to point out your flushed cheeks?" she quietly stated.

"Not the first," he said, taking a deep breath.

"Or the dark rings around your eyes?" she said, her voice growing softer.

"Nope," he groaned.

"Or that knotted-up tangle on top of your head?" whispered Joanna, leaning back and peering at her friend with a sideways glance.

"My hair? What's wrong with my hair?" he said, gently patting the bramble atop his head. "Wait! What? Ah, I forgot to oil after the shower this morning. Real nice."

"It's okay. I think it's a good look. Older and more rugged," she said, holding back a laugh.

"A good look?" he replied. "Have you ever seen a more unkempt WAFE?"

"Good point. But it reminds me of something too...an outdoor event, a past challenge, or maybe some training that didn't go as planned." Joanna zoned out, staring at her tray in silence until a crash of pans in the kitchen brought her back to the cafeteria.

"The fall Sojourn?" said Heschel, taking a bite of his vitabread before spitting it discreetly into his hand. "Whoa! That may be the stalest, mustiest vitabread I've had around here in...well...ever. Don't tell me you already ate yours?"

Joanna unzipped a small carryall at her side. She had used it the previous semester to hold her soldering gun, flux, and a small tube of solder for her electronic repairs session. A green-tinged slice of crumbled vitabread was stuffed inside.

Heschel shook his head.

"That's it! Your hair reminds me of the Sojourn, only I still don't remember anything about it," she said, quickly zipping the pouch. If a monitor saw the bread, no doubt she'd be accused of sneaking extra.

"Come to think of it, the rations around here haven't quite been the same since that Sojourn, either," said Heschel, endlessly stirring the yellowed yogurt in an unusually small cup. "And there's something else too."

Joanna slowly sipped her water, watching the monitors watch her.

"Ming said something unusual heading into the first session."

"Chih-ming?" she said, sipping her room temperature water.

"Of course," his voice squeaked. "There's only one Chih-ming, isn't there?"

"Well, yeah, I guess so. There's only one of each of us, really. I don't think there's another Joanna on the compound. Or another Heschel. Or another Charlie..." Joanna trailed off as she spoke that last name out loud.

"Why did you say that?" Heschel asked, half standing and raising his voice.

"Charlie?" she repeated, spilling water as she set it down.

"Chih asked me about them this morning. And now you. Who are they? I don't know anyone on the entire compound with that name. Do you?"

Joanna pulled her friend down with a thud, then kicked him in the shin with her heel. "Take this and eat it," she said, handing him the expired yogurt. "I don't know what's gotten into you, but in case you hadn't noticed, every monitor here has been watching us since we arrived. I kinda have this weird feeling that they've been watching us for months, only I'm just now realizing it."

Heschel looked around the room. He felt unsettled as well but dismissed it. "Who's Charlie? Do you know, or is it more like trying to remember a dream after you wake? Familiar yet empty," whispered Heschel, awkwardly dropping into his seat.

"I guess I don't know," she said, pushing the yogurt into his hand. "I feel like I'm just now waking up from a long nap, and some things are different. Like this food."

As soon as Heschel stuck the spoonful of sour yogurt into his mouth, the fire alarm went off. One-hundred and twenty decibels of mind-shaking electronic squawking coupled with flashing lights and shouting monitors filled the room. In a well-trained and orderly fashion, all the students rose to their feet, left their moldy vitabread on their trays, then marched single file down the hall, through the main entrance, and into the courtyard.

Everyone but Heschel and Joanna.

3 Deplorable

The two Observers ended up at the back of the long line in the rear of the cafeteria after the alarm went off. They hadn't intended to be the last in line, but something compelled them to rise a little later than the rest, walk a bit slower, and avoid eye contact with other students. It was a familiar feeling, even comforting, though unexplainable.

"Pssst. Hesch! Heschel, back here!"

The voice was shrill, even as a whisper, as if someone was under incredible pressure.

"Joanna! Hurry before they notice you haven't left with the others."

Heschel grabbed Joanna's upper arm, pulling in the

direction of the voice. Before their numerous rounds of re-education, Joanna wouldn't have resisted. But now, without a rational basis for wild trust in a moment of mystery, she hesitated.

"Don't you sense it?" Heschel asked.

"Who is it? Why are we listening? I feel something, but fear is definitely topping the list of reasonable responses right now," she said, continuing to pull back.

"I see it, don't you?" Heschel said, his voice rising. "The glow. I remember now. I don't know who's back there, but I remember the light, that faint pulsing. How could I forget?"

One step at a time, they moved closer to the voice calling them.

"It's you," said the man, hidden inside a storage closet in the back wing of the cafeteria. "I can't believe it worked! I can't believe it led me straight to you. Of the hundreds of students in this cursed re-education camp, it brought me right here."

The two students froze outside the propped-open closet door.

"You know who we are?" asked Joanna, her voice shaking. "What do you mean it led you here? Why are you dressed like that?"

Heschel slowly stepped forward as though he were in a trance. Reaching for the door, he gently pulled it open to shed some light on the figure. The man who stepped forward was unlike anyone they'd ever met. To be fair, they'd never actually met anyone from beyond the camp except for a few Anti-Libertas leaders from time to time.

His clothes were from some ancient era, clearly handmade. His threadbare button-up shirt was made of flannel and worn to death, while his pants were a heavy material, dyed blue, and ripped to shreds over the knees with patches covering his thighs and calves. He had a well-worn leather side bag slung over his shoulder, crisscrossing his chest. A stretched thin winter hat covered his head. Long tangled dreadlocks hanging well below the approved compound length spilled out from underneath. And his dark tan face was half-covered with an old linen scarf which donned a familiar symbol the two students immediately recognized.

Letting out a deep sigh, the wild-looking creature of a man reached forward as he stepped from the closet.

Joanna's eyes grew wide at his sudden movement. Panicking, she yanked her arm from Heschel's grip. She screamed so loud and shrill that both Heschel and the wild man lurched forward, covering their ears, while Joanna stumbled backward, tripping over her feet and falling onto her side.

"Take it, man! Take it now!" cried the wild being as he pulled an outdated USB flash drive from his leather bag and thrust it in Heschel's direction.

Heschel stared at the memory drive waving in front of him. He looked back at Joanna lying on the floor behind him, yelling and pointing across the cafeteria. He looked across the room at the flood of deputized monitors heading their way at full speed. Everything was moving in slow motion. Voices were muffled as though underwater. And the glow was there, but it wasn't just an orb as it had been in the past. It was everywhere. The whole room glowed, hazy and soft, like trying to see after swimming underwater with your eyes open.

"We knew you were awake. Now don't stop until you've followed the chain. Don't stop!" commanded the wild man, tucking the flash drive into Heschel's pocket before shoving him to the floor beside Joanna and out of the path of the coming onslaught. Before the students could respond, the monitors leaped into the air, tackling the ominous character without restraint.

"You two," said a white-haired monitor with a rich foreign accent overseeing the charge, "stay where you are. You are in shock from the gas leak in the kitchen. We'll take you to the infirmary to assess your condition as soon as this confused kitchen porter is cared for."

 ## 4 I Remember Now

The air was crisp in the shade of the giant oak. The lead monitor was on a mission, traversing the courtyard between the cafeteria and The Adavis Center for Progress in record time.

"Heschel, are you…." Joanna began before being cut off by the monitor squeezing her arm extra tight.

Do you remember where I first felt the presence of the glow? Heschel said with an out-of-place smile amid the swarm of deputized monitors.

Joanna looked at him wide-eyed and mouthed, "How am I hearing you?"

It was in the re-education room, deep down in my

subconscious, or my gut, only deeper and fuller. A sort of meta-peace covered the entire ordeal like I imagine a fleece blanket would feel in the heart of winter. I had forgotten about it. Heschel looked up as they passed the oak tree in the courtyard's center. He watched a handful of crows descend above the uppermost branches, returning with the spring. *I felt it again. I saw it in the cafeteria. It covered everything. Everyone. I think that crazy person back there, whoever they are, is right. It led them to us because we have something to accomplish.*

"But why us?" Joanna pressed, stopping briefly and pulling away from the monitor. "I have no idea what's going on? Or what you and I have to do with it all. I don't remember!"

At the screeching command of the white-haired monitor, the squad suddenly halted. Throwing Heschel to the ground, they encircled the students. Quick as soldiers, they dislodged shock rifles from their leather holsters and fixed their aim on each Observer. Neither student had ever witnessed a shock rifle aimed at another human outside of training.

Supernaturally calm, Heschel deliberately looked each monitor in the eye around the circle. He felt older. He felt their confusion. He watched as the glow began to illuminate the squad, one by one, like an undefined ring of fire consuming their bodies. *Joanna, it'll be okay. They won't get hurt.*

How do you know? she replied. *What's happening?*

Heschel closed his eyes. Lying on his side, he awkwardly pulled his arm from beneath him and turned the palms of his hands to the sky. Then, without saying a word and with no weapon in his possession, he cupped his hands together. The fear on Joanna's face caught the squad's attention, who turned their focus to the ball of light beginning to emanate from within Heschel's hands.

"Lieutenant? You're going to want to see this!" hollered one of the monitors standing over Heschel.

Before she could respond, Heschel gently opened his cupped hands, releasing a micro-singularity of glowing molten energy. Concentric rings of light flashed around the entire group with a pressure that forced them backward and down to the ground. They weren't blown back as though an explosion had detonated. No, it was silent and controlled. The light rings pressed the squad down, as though gravity had increased, but only on the circle of monitors.

"Keep them in your sights," barked the lead monitor as she turned to find her team fastened to the ground. Before she could utter another command, a small orb rose from the center of the commotion. At first, it appeared as though it were going to return to Heschel. Then, as though discovering a better plan, the orb raced directly toward the lieutenant's face, paused in a violent spasm, then disappeared within itself in a spectacular solar flash.

The squad could only watch, helplessly pinned to the

concrete path. Their drab gray uniforms were riddled with char marks as though sprayed with hot ash. And their gloss-black metal rifle shafts had warped with snakelike bends as though impacted by a raging forge.

Joanna, palms-sweating and jittery, stared at her friend now lying with his head on the ground and unconscious.

"I can't see," muttered the white-haired lieutenant. "I CAN'T SEE ANYTHING!"

 **5 Dr. Breach**

"**C**-40 on red," ordered Principal Chicanery. "Catch the virus before it spreads." He was leaning against the wall behind the administrative desk inside the re-education center. With folded arms, he watched the aids rush back and forth. Empty beds rolled in from the infirmary. Makeshift stations were formed on rolling storage carts. Intravenous bags filled with a refined solution designed for memory redefinition were hung on IV stands and shared between patients.

"Principal Chicanery, we've never l-l-locked-down on r-r-red before—n-n-n-not outside of a training drill. There will be questions. No doubt there were witnesses in the c-c-c-courtyard!" Principal Chicanery's assistant spoke fast. Their face flushed cherry red. Beads of sweat stopped along their regulation hairline just above the forehead.

"Lock it down. I want every subject in their assigned room—staff included. In several minutes I'll go live on Stream with the proper narrative," he said somberly. A tone he had rehearsed in order to cut through even the most chaotic scene.

"Ten monitors, two students, and one lieutenant," shouted the lead doctor working to distribute the proper dose of IV solution to the appropriate biological patient.

"We're going to need restraints over here!" yelled a very petite aid wrestling with the much more imposing lieutenant.

"I am not a subject here. I developed that solution and will *not* be putting that toxin into my bloodstream! Do you hear me, Chicanery?" Though unable to see, the lieutenant violently tossed the aid to the floor. Swinging her feet from the bed, she kicked the aide in the nose while pulling another nurse overtop the mattress and onto the monitor laying nervously beside her.

The lieutenant's fight spread like an airborne virus. Within minutes each of the monitors began to panic, shout, and wrestle with the aids attempting to insert needles into their veins.

"You can't do this to me!" screamed the lieutenant with a

contempt typically reserved for Deplorables. "You begged me to take on this catastrophe! You asked me to handle your little uprising! I'll have you court-martialed for this, Chicanery!"

"To be fair," said the principal, "I *can* do this. As for the court-marshaling, it's standard practice that the plaintiff, at the very least, remembers the crime committed to accuse the defendant in the first place. As you can see, I'm not too worried."

The back door of the room flew open. In rushed two-dozen monitors carrying shock rifles who began swinging them wildly. It was an unfair fight with two to three monitors stomping, punching, shocking, and ultimately restraining their fellow monitors. Heschel and Joanna, though having been patiently lying in their beds, were nonetheless shocked and secured amidst the uproar.

The electrical pulses were excruciating. The first sensation upon contact with the prongs was the mildest, like the bite of a wild wolf fighting for its life. Next, a deadening throb of electricity rushed through the limb, as if a lightning strike were injected directly beneath the skin and burning to get out. Immediately after, the victim would lose control of their muscles, releasing their bowels without any ability to restrain themselves. Finally, their brains would shut down in order to protect other bodily systems from the voltage.

Once the screaming had stopped, and the room was filled

with little more than the sound of groaning, feet shuffling, and restocking, Principal Chicanery ordered the excess monitors to leave. Without a word, he returned to his office in Chagrin Center to concoct a more believable storyline to share on Stream.

"That's six XY and seven XX patients, am I correct? Make sure you confirm before starting the drip. No mistakes, people!" said Dr. Breach, immediately returning to work. "XY and XX subjects respond differently to the solution. It's been an incredibly unsettling afternoon with all this commotion, I feel obligated to keep us focused. The solution is a new addition, so take a breath and do it right." Hundreds of trials and thousands of real-time uses at distant compounds had proven this true. Male and female subjects responded differently to the chemical compounds. To mix them up could cause irreversible harm to the patient, particularly a developing student. And permanently altering a student's biological or mental design was a form of cruelty few but the Anti-Libertas leadership could stomach.

As each patient succumbed to the mildly tranquilizing compounds built into the solution, an aide would affix a headset connected to memory training material and begin the re-education loop. One by one, each member joined in the subconscious pursuit of progressive unity.

An hour into the memory training, Dr. Breach's device signaled a call. "Yes, Principal Chicanery, what can I help you with?"

"Dr. Breach, you look tired. Difficult work, isn't it? Listen, I'm concerned about our two rebellious students, aren't you?" he confided, falling silent on the screen with an uncomfortable smirk.

"Well…I…I think we just need more time and…" she began, squirming in her chair and clearing her throat.

"It's a complete loss. The lieutenant has failed us with that weak solution," he said, his voice rising with impatience. "I want you to double dose the students. I want you to cross biologically designed compounds, and I want you to do the same to Lieutenant Kresreb while you're at it. Give them everything you've got!"

"Principal Chicanery," she whispered, knowing the weight of her next few words, "it might…it might kill them."

"One more thing," he said, glossing over her fears. "Let's try speeding up the loop. A little dysphoric vertigo goes a long way don't you think?"

"I have no idea what effect that will have on their minds," she said, stepping back while nervously rubbing her forehead. "There are too many unknowns to investigate in one session. I need time…and data…and assistance… and…."

"Progress before people, Dr. Breach. Don't let me down."

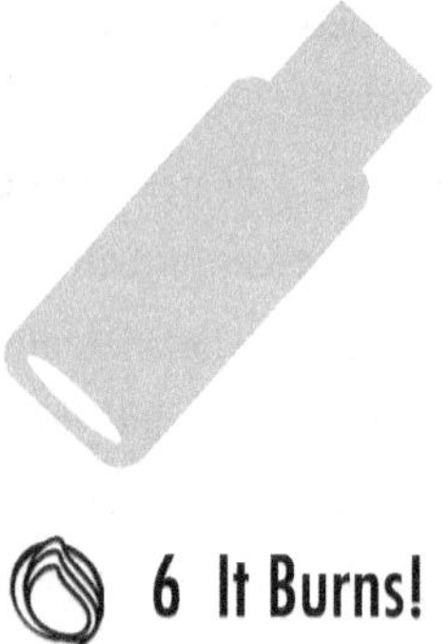

6 It Burns!

Attention staff and student body at the unparalleled Compound 40. Principal Chicanery's voice was calm and controlled. He was a master of presentation.

Chih-ming had just arrived at his third session of the day when his device lit up—along with every other device and screen in the room. The principal had groomed the entire compound to pause when he appeared on Stream. And they obeyed without fail. It was reflexive attention more than it was an honorable salute. But it was effective.

You may have heard rumors about some exciting events happening around our beloved compound this afternoon. Well, I want to assure you that these successful training exercises have come to an end, and the students involved in this pre-planned experiment are safe and secure, just as we plan on keeping each and every one of you.

Chih-ming had heard about the disarray in the courtyard. Everyone had heard. While he was relieved that he hadn't witnessed the chaotic events, Chih-ming was instinctively disappointed that, once again, he wasn't a part of it either. As the day went on, he not only overheard accounts of what supposedly took place in the cafeteria but also watched half a dozen silly reenactments of what took place in the courtyard—slow-motion replays with valiant monitors and dramatic death scenes. Without much thought, a stinging sensation began to pierce his chest. The more he brooded on the day's mysterious events, his time with Charlie, and his awkward conversation with Heschel that morning, the more his chest burned.

If that weren't enough, rumors of explosions in dorms, gunfights along the edge, and sabotaged surveillance equipment were spreading like an airborne virus. After all, Compound 40 was small, and no matter how obedient the student body continued to be, they were still students. And students instinctively spread really good-bad gossip. The more elaborate the story, the deeper the sting. But by the end of the day, it had subsided. Not wanting to make a fuss, he avoided the infirmary and went on with his evening routine.

It was another two days before Chih-ming was convinced that Heschel had something to do with the so-called training exercise.

At first, it was simple connect-the-dots reasoning. His morning session instructor, a session he shared with Heschel, mentioned in passing that Heschel would be out for several days due to an impromptu Wide Awake training. Believable? Sure. Normal? Sort of. A little suspicious? Absolutely.

It wasn't until the third day, however, that Chih's doubts were erased. After the fourth and final session of the day, he spent his break studying in the courtyard before dinner. *I've never seen so many students hanging around out here in the cold!* he thought. *Seems everyone wants in on the strange activity.* After his meager snack of stale vitabread and sugar water, he headed back to his flat. As he reached his floor, a light pressure began to build in his chest. Pushing open his room door, he saw his roommate sitting perfectly still, sweating and shaking. They were being questioned by two deputized monitors and oblivious to Chih's arrival. It was clear they had been at it for a while. The burning in his chest exploded. He wanted to run, but whether it was his training or the burning, he calmly and obediently stayed put.

"Have a seat," said one of the monitors turning toward Chih. "You're next."

Next? he thought. *Sounds more like a threat than an invitation.*

Upon completion, his roommate was asked to keep their discussion a secret for security reasons. Before Chih could say a word, they ushered his roommate out of the room, closed the door, then sat down across from Chih.

The conversation was brief since Chih had no information to share. His device proved his location away from the activity during the chaos. "Is it true that you spoke with a fellow Observer named Heschel that morning?"

"Yes," said Chih-ming, sweat beginning to build beneath his regulation cut mop of straight, black hair. Their eyes asked for more detail.

"Um…well…I thought they looked ill," he sputtered. "I asked if they had been to the infirmary for a check-up."

"A check-up. That's all?" said the monitor, leaning forward, purposely invading Chih-ming's personal bubble. They froze in place for what felt like an hour. Both monitors relentlessly stared him down until he bowed his head in submission. "It would be wise to keep this interaction between the three of us," said the elder monitor nearly forehead to forehead with Chih, who was sweating profusely. Without another word, the monitors departed.

The burning in his chest had spread to his neck and down into his shoulders. It was clear Heschel was at the center of the mystery. It was also clear that something was compelling him to get involved.

What have I gotten myself into? I shouldn't have

instigated things with Heschel. Chih fell back onto his bed. *I helped Charlie out, and he disappeared. Now Heschel is gone, and who knows who else is wrapped up in this.* He rolled onto his side and pulled the pillow over his head. *My insides feel like lava. Is this what emotion feels like? No way, it's gotta be the vitabread.* Too tired to try and make sense of it, Chih-ming dozed off.

His room was dark and abnormally cold when he awoke. The burning that had been spreading throughout his body had recoiled back into his chest, only now it felt like something prodding him to move—to act. Silently, not wanting to disturb his sleeping roommate, Chih carefully removed the card from his device—something he'd done hundreds of times. Slipping from his bed, he crept across the floor, opened the door, and stepped into the dim hall eerily aglow with red emergency lights. Again, his midnight adventures to the museum had become so routine that the process shouldn't have phased him. Yet this time, it was different. The tug in his chest was pulling him in a new direction. He usually turned right. This time he turned left. He typically went down the stairs at the north end of the dorm. This time he went down the stairs on the southern end. Normally he'd sneak between buildings in a well-orchestrated dance of hide-and-seek with the monitors and cameras across the compound. This time, however, he moved from one floor to the next, not knowing which door or flat he was being led to.

Then he saw it—the glow.

His heart stopped along with his feet. Fire flared up within his chest again. *Someone else is awake. No one is ever awake this late. Heschel? Heschel's back! He's gotta be.* Without a second to lose, Chih took off down the hall, pausing directly in front of Heschel and Joanna's flat. The light shone brighter through the cracks along the edge of the door. Before he could touch the handle, the door swung open. Something pulled him inside.

"Heschel! You're..." The relief Chih felt dissolved. The room was dark. It was quiet. And it was very cold.

7 Missing Days

Following the first twenty-four hours, the monitors were evaluated, fed a new narrative, and released. The new story would settle in while the actual event would fade into nothing more than a dream—a confusing array of warped memories too embarrassing to discuss with anyone else on the compound.

Lieutenant Kresreb spent two days absorbing the memory-distorting solution. It was a chaotic forty-eight-hour sprint as the two biologically assigned blends coursed through her veins. One minute her heart rate would spike, and the next, it would flatline. Dr. Breach ran ragged with little sleep. There was too much data to process and too little time to prepare for each emergency. And with two more students to stabilize across the room, the doctor was simply spent.

After forty-eight hours of physical and mental exhaustion, Lieutenant Kresreb's condition stabilized. Blood, breathing, pulse, and reflex tests were repeated in those final hours. The findings were recorded, as required, and, finally, Lieutenant Kresreb left to spend another day regaining her strength while learning the narrative under supervised care in the infirmary.

For two more days, Heschel and Joanna absorbed the combined IV compounds and the re-education loop at two times the speed. Their groaning finally subsided in the late hours of the fourth night. Though exhausted, Dr. Breach had filled a file worth of notes on their intense reactions. She was also meticulous, recording everything following that first drip of the IV. She noted the stages of Joanna's screaming as the fluid appeared to burn its way through her veins like lava across a forest floor. Or Heschel's rigor mortis-like muscle response on the morning of the third day. And their simultaneous bouts of labored breathing in the middle of entirely different episodes, as though something supernatural would temporarily unite them in their subconscious struggle for life. Fevers, and rashes, and bruising, and swelling, and sweating, and moaning, and seizures, and, well, anything that could happen to a heart, mind, body, and spirit under pressure happened in that re-education room over those five days.

On the fifth and final day, Dr. Breach drew blood one last time from each of their arms. The doctor immediately processed the specimens just as she had been doing from day one. This time, however, something was different.

"Principal Chicanery, I...you...I think you're going to want to see this," she said, speaking fast into her device and shaking. "Their blood, it's, well...it's adapted."

"They're still alive then, eh? Good, good, good," he said. "What does that mean, *adapted*?"

"It, um, appears as though the solution has functioned like a vaccine. Their bodies have begun to reject the compound entirely as a result of combining the XY and XX solutions," she said, terrified at what this discovery might mean to The Chamber. More scared, however, to share those findings with Chicanery. "We may have just inoculated them against our re-education, but we won't know until they're fully awake and strong enough to test."

"Don't do anything until I arrive. I want to be there when you remove them from the treatment. I want to look into their clueless eyes the moment they wake." Principal Chicanery ended the call with a smirk. A sort of sinister smile that, for the first time in Dr. Breach's tenure at Compound 40, had a physical effect on her mood—an unsettling inner fear that gave birth to what ancient theologians and philosophers called an ethical dilemma. And it seemed to travel straight to her stomach.

Principal Chicanery left his office with a renewed sense of control. It wasn't that he had everything figured out. No, quite the opposite. An immunity to the re-education process would severely set back the Anti-Libertas world vision. Principal Chicanery was a fighter. He rose to power within The Chamber of Trust fast and not without bloody competition. He preferred a challenge. And being backed into a corner with no clear path forward stirred that fighting spirit within him.

He decided to take the stairs down from the third story. His heart was racing, and he was feeling scrappy. Taking a detour into the heart of Chagrin Center, he entered the main hall, the center of justice at Compound 40. Pausing beneath the newly renovated stained-glass dome high above, he took a deep breath, closed his eyes, and exhaled long and slowly.

"This is it," he whispered to the glow, the past shadows, and the empty wooden pews encircling the hall. "This is the beginning of the end. If these insecure little zealots are the best you have, well, it's safe to say I'm simply witnessing the last gasps of an ancient belief dying a disgraceful death. But don't worry. I'll usher you and your glowing ones out in style."

"Principal Chicanery, we need your eyes on something immediately," said a monitor, quickly entering a set of doors next to the stage.

The principal, unphased by the interruption, smiled, nodded, and made his way toward the exit. "Yes, I'm aware. I was on my way to the re-education center now."

"No, not the re-education room," said the monitor, short of breath. "The hot spot. The Deplorable."

The hot spot added another layer of secrecy to Compound 40. Situated alongside the re-education room, the hot spot was designed for those rare and less desirable interactions with unruly characters. It was a fraction of the size of the re-education room and outfitted to perform the same tasks along with a few additional sinister deeds.

Principal Chicanery's lips pursed as his usually upbeat walk stiffened. "Have they escaped?"

"No, they're just as we left them," replied the monitor leading the way. "It's just that we followed your newly revised protocol with the memory solution, and, well, something's happened."

"Immunized," said Chicanery, slowing his pace near the entrance to The Adavis Center for Progress.

"Yes," said the monitor. "How did you know?"

"I'll be there shortly," he muttered, ignoring the monitor's shock. "I'm going to the source."

Dr. Breach met him in the hallway, scanned her device to unlock the secure re-education door, then rushed in behind him, eager to shed some light on her findings. She was beginning to transfer the students' charts to the main screen behind the desk when the lights in the room flickered.

"So this is how you're going to play the game, is it?" Chicanery murmered. Turning from Dr. Breach, he began to make his way toward Heschel, bumping into the beds, IV stands, and supply carts as he grew increasingly disoriented from the strobing lights.

"Principal?" Dr. Breach shouted. "Principal Chicanery!" Crouching low next to the desk, she called for his attention. "What's going on? What's that sound? Are we under attack?"

The humming noise was familiar to the elder statesman.

"It's the death throes of a former empire spitting up blood and crying out in shame!" he shouted as the humming crackled and the room began to tremble.

You won't win. You can't win. I'm ending this today. Now! he thought, glaring at the helpless students. Chicanery grabbed the edge of Heschel's bed and pulled a thin knife from his pocket. The wooden scales were well worn with a metal tag on one side that read **Old Timer.** *Chicanery* was carved into the handle on the opposite side, though now missing letters, worn out from use. The narrow blade wasn't more than three inches long, yet it was just as sharp as the day his grandfather bought it.

Dr. Breach couldn't believe what she was witnessing. The strobing lights, the head-pounding noise without a source, the shaking floor, and Principal Chicanery, the czar of equality, preparing to personally harm an unconscious student. Terrified, she crawled to the exit and attempted to scan her device over and over on the reader. With each flicker of the light and every tremor, the power to the security system came and went. After several attempts, the green light flashed. Just as she pulled on the handle, a force from the outside violently thrust inward. The door swung open with a vengeance slamming into the side of her head and knocking her unconscious. Pushing her out of the way, several deputized monitors who had been kicking at the door since the chaos began rushed in, grabbed the manic principal before he could act, and carried him off against his will. Two monitors picked up Dr. Breach as they exited and then disappeared down the hall.

The uproar immediately stopped.

Heschel sat up, removed the headset, pulled the IV from his arm, and stepped down from his bed. Immediately he began to assist Joanna, who was still passed out on the disheveled bed next to his.

It's time to wake up. It's over. I remember now, don't you? Charlie and Maria. I know where we hid the relic. I saw them too. That family. My family! At least, I think they were. I guess I don't remember everything yet. It's time to wake up, Joanna. We have work to do, but we need to play their game. We need to convince Chicanery that we're renewed creatures. That we're re-educated and eager to obey. We need to become invisible gray uniforms in a gray ocean until it…until the glow leads us to whatever's next.

35

 ## 8 Another Clue

Heschel and Joanna's room looked like no one had stepped foot in there in days. And the bright light that had been emanating from the room? Gone. Chih-ming freaked out.

"H...H...Hello?" he said, his voice quivering. *What on the edge is going on tonight?* he thought, turning in circles and searching for any sign of life.

"Someone had a flashlight in here a minute ago," he muttered as fear slowly morphed into frustration. "Someone opened that door before I even touched it. I'm not crazy!"

His back was to the door, standing between the beds,

when a low hum rose behind him.

"Someone pulled me into this room!" he growled, whipping around the door. "I may not be leadership material, but I'm not a fool."

Like a spooked animal hunched over and ready to pounce, he inched forward. His eyes and ears strained to find the source of the unsettling buzz. One slow step after another, his long legs seemed to glide across the sterile floor. Chih was about to reach for the door handle when he caught a familiar but strange sight out of the corner of his right eye. It was the glow. *I've seen this before. Maybe something like it. That's right! On the dark ledger, when I was searching out clues for Charlie. Sheesh! I thought the pixels on the screen were freaking out, but they weren't. It was this…this glow. It was leading me.*

A soft, yellow light illuminated from behind the standard-issue shelf right next to him. At first, he thought a malfunctioning nightlight might be the culprit—though the burning in his chest told him otherwise. Slowly he turned toward the glow and grabbed hold of the little cabinet, hoping to explain the source of the flickering light.

Whatever's leading me on this squirrel chase is having a good laugh right about now, he thought, feeling pretty foolish at all the creeping and clamoring. Chih closed his eyes, counted to three, then pulled the stand away from the wall. A radiant light washed over the room.

"It's not a nightlight! It's not a nightlight!" he cried, stumbling back against the wall. The same force that had pulled him into the room now yanked him low to the ground directly in front of the hidden cubby. The force was so powerful and sudden that he threw his hands up to brace himself from a head-on collision with the wall. Heart thumping and chest burning, Chih opened his eyes to find a rectangular-shaped crevice in the wall beaming with light. *A hidden compartment? I wonder if Hesch knows about this? He has to. It's... It's sooo obvious.*

Nervously, Chih-ming ran his hands along the glowing seam in search of a handle. After several rounds without luck, he applied a little pressure until finally, feeling a mechanical pop, the hidden door swung open as a magnetic latch was released. Once again, light poured from the secret nook causing him to flinch and recoil from the incredible glare. *Is this really happening? Nope. I don't believe it. These things don't happen to me. I'm just a simple transistor, not a motherboard. The Chamber would've chosen me by now if I had the qualities of a leader...right?*

Shielding his eyes, Chih boldly reached into the mysterious cavity. Feeling around, he grabbed hold of the only item hidden within. It was heavier than he anticipated, though not much to look at. Immediately the buzzing sound fizzled, and the blazing light burned out. Shaky and cold, the young Observer sat silently cradling the mysterious container.

Charlie, what did you get me into? The box was made of a hard yet flimsy green plastic, like his old session supply bin when he was a Seeker. The contents bounced around without any support. The sort of storage that drove Chih crazy. He was very particular about the items in his care. Order and organization. It's why he felt at home in the blockchain behind Stream. Digital order. Code. Binary transactions. Everything in its place and running as it was designed. Charlie, however, threw a wrench in his ordered rhythm.

"There's absolutely no turning back if I open this, is there?" he mumbled, debating on whether or not it was finally time to run, though he doubted the burning in his chest and the invisible tug would let him off the hook. "This is it—time to level-up Ming. You already know more than you should. That something's off the chain. Open it! Let's do this!"

Chih gripped the edge of the plastic lid, held his breath, squeezed tight, then popped the top open like a curious child with a surprise gift.

That's it? That's the ancient relic Charlie gushed over? The one he couldn't bring to the library? Chih picked up the small broken tablet, turning it over and over again, he was thoroughly unimpressed. *It's a dirty ole broken rock. And what's this?* he wondered, rummaging through the box. *Scraps of paper and trinkets? This is why that creepy orb led me here?*

Disappointed, he stared out the window into the clear, star-filled sky. Not nearly as impressed as the others, Chih inspected the stone the way a two-year-old might a bar of gold. After concluding that he and Charlie must have already uncovered what clues it had to offer, he carelessly shoved it into an oversized pocket in his uniform. Tapping the flashlight app, he set his device off to the side, shining into the box in order to explore the contents more freely. Inside he found a half-dozen scraps of paper faded and torn with notes scribbled across them. He found some polished stones with odd symbols he had never seen before crudely carved into them. Symbols that didn't seem to match anything on the tablet. There were a couple of blue and orange plastic cards, each with a dark magnetic strip down the backside along with names and codes punched into the front that he couldn't quite decipher. *Outdated identification cards, I guess. Stolen from the museum?*

Chih was ready to pack it up when the invisible force nudged his hand toward the scraps of paper like a marionette. "What on the edge!" he shrieked, pulling his arm back only to hit his funny bone on the wall behind him. *I don't want to be rude, invisible-bully-thing, but you're really creeping me out! Could you maybe stop grabbing me and, you know, just glow or give a little whisper instead?*

"Yeesss," whispered a gentle voice into his ear with an uncomfortable warmth. The response was clear and close yet seemed to emanate from a long distance away, as though from another dimension.

"No! No! No! NOOO!" he stuttered in full panic mode like someone scrambling to scrape a spider from their neck. Dropping the box, he lurched forward, smacking his forehead on the corner of the small shelf. "I was wrong! I was wrong! Don't whisper. Nudge. NUDGE! That was absolutely the most horrifying thing I've ever heard. What's going on around here?"

Chih-ming sat hunched over, brushing invisible spider webs from his ear and neck until he could breathe steady and sure. Once again, the burning in his chest began to rise. This time, however, it felt different. He felt a peace that seemed to cut through the confusion and fear. Inner courage to sit up straight, trust the process and finish the mission with clarity and confidence.

Of all things to feel after such an unsettling event—angry, scared, annoyed, defeated—Chih felt older, a bit stronger, and, for the first time as a gray cog in the compound machine, he felt like he had a purpose.

With a deep breath, he set to work. The first few notes didn't catch his attention. However, the last two gave him goosebumps.

The first scrap was a pencil sketch of what looked like the end cap, or leg, of an old wooden bench. Bringing the faded paper closer to the light, Chih saw what appeared to be a rectangular shape drawn on one leg of the pew, shaded in, and etched with several ancient symbols. *Where on the edge is there an elaborately carved wooden pew on the compound?*

"I've seen these before. These are some of the symbols Charlie and I translated," he mumbled, fumbling with the stone from his pocket in a hurry to check it over. "There it is! Those symbols are on this tablet. But why? What does one have to do with the other? And if I made this connection in just a few minutes, no doubt Heschel has too. He's probably already found the pews. But then again, what if he hasn't?"

Chih sat back, letting the discovery sink in before moving on to the final note.

To: H & J

Believe it or not, you're reading a note written by YOU. You've been re-educated. Oh, and you're probably being watched by Principal Chicanery and any number of his student-monitor spies. Here's the deal, we buried the other half of the tablet along the edge under the north side of the Microcachrys tetragona, 200 feet east of the falls. Trust the glow. It'll know what to do.   - From: H & J

Chih set the paper scrap down on his lap, put his face in his hands, and leaned back against the wall. *It just keeps getting weirder.* Taking a few deep breaths, he began to pack up the odds and ends when he heard the sound of a door closing, followed by crisp footsteps heading towards him down the hall.

Spry as a rabbit and trying not to hyperventilate, he tucked everything but the sketch, the note from H & J, and the relic into the box, placed it in the cubby, pushed the door closed until the magnet caught, then slid the shelf back into place. He had just turned off his flashlight when the steps came to a complete stop on the other side of the door. His heart beat so loud he was convinced the monitor, or whoever it was, could hear it through the door.

After thirty agonizing seconds, Chih watched as the door handle turned in slow motion. His throat closed as he curled into an upright fetal position directly behind the door. It opened just enough for an adult standing sideways to slip inside. Chih didn't move a muscle. He could see the nose of the monitor staring directly forward into the room though not entering fully. "These students will never learn," they said with a sinister chuckle before stepping back into the hall, releasing the door to slowly close on its own.

Looks like I know what I'm doing tomorrow night. First, I'm gonna find out what a Mic...Micro...cocharoachero... tetragonicus is. Then I'm gonna find that other piece of the tablet. Then I'm gonna take a nap.

 9 Follow the Leader

"We're gonna lose it, Hesch," Joanna whispered, crouching low to the floor. It had been a month since their chaotic ride in the re-education room. A month since Chih had been drawn toward the relics and notes. The paranoid atmosphere around the compound had cooled, though security remained particularly heavy. Wherever they went, whichever session they attended, Kresreb and her committed troop of deputized monitors were stationed nearby.

Heschel stared down the dark hall. Red emergency lights illuminated the intersection just ahead, right where the orb had ventured left down a short tributary.

"We have five minutes until the next patrol passes through," she said, her voice anxiously rising.

"Relax. We have all the time we need," said Heschel, mapping out the possible location the glow might be leading them.

"We've been trying to get into this building for the past month. Don't let it out of your sight, Hesch. We already missed our chance to find the second half of the tablet. We can't afford to miss out on this too." Joanna stood behind him, leaned against the cold block wall, and sighed deeply.

Grabbing her hand, he gently tugged until she slid back down to a crouching position. "The glow hasn't abandoned us yet, has it? Look, I don't know what happened to the relic we buried. Someone got to it before us, Chicanery or Kresreb, but we can't give up. After all we've been through, I'm not gonna ignore the glow or this burning in my chest. Are you?"

Thin tears rolled down her cheeks as she dropped her head into her arms folded across the tops of her knees.

"Hesch, I'm afraid. I don't see things as clearly as you do. I mean, the glow in the re-education room...it showed me things about the past, not the future," she said, looking up at an Anti-Libertas poster on the wall across from them and letting the tears fall. *To risk the loss of progress is to reap regress.* She read it several times, then shook her head in anger. Her emotions had begun to take the lead since that wild event.

Heschel paused, then crawled back to meet her. His cheeks flushed as he crouched against the wall shoulder to shoulder. For a moment, they sat in silence. The building felt empty, cold, and stale, yet, like Chih, the burning in his chest offered more peace than fear.

"Did you see what I saw back there? You know, about your own past," he said, nearly whispering, looking down at his hands. "Before they brought us here."

"Like Maria?" Joanna replied, turning toward him. She watched him look over his hands, tap his knuckles, and follow the creases on his palms. It was a strange habit he had only recently picked up.

"Yeah, like Maria."

"I saw what must have been a person like me. The whisper beneath the images called it a woman, like you said before—a mother. My mother, I guess. And there was one like you there. My father? And there were others like me, at least they looked like me when I was little, and they were running and playing." Joanna began to relax her shoulders as she imagined those three little girls laughing and hugging.

"The first time I saw them, that first trip at the start of this whole mess, they were like shadows behind a foggy window," Hesch whispered. "I felt like running to them, but it passed before I could move. That's when I saw other humans all dressed up, the ones I told you about before," he said, taking a deep breath and dropping his head back against the wall. "This time, the fog was gone, and they were looking right at me. He was tall and bald, dark and skinny like me. Only more muscular. Hard to believe...I know." Grinning wide and chuckling, he flexed his average -size biceps hidden beneath the baggy uniform.

Joanna snorted a laugh.

"She was short, stout, and smiley. Then poof! Lost in a kaleidoscope of sights and sounds."

"He and she. Father and mother. We're more than XX and XY, aren't we?" she said, choking down a deep bellow.

"We've known it this whole time," he said, raising his voice. "Plain as day and night, it's a secret *waaay* out in the open. Only now we have the language to describe the bio-mental differences we've always talked around. And it feels right. Things seem clearer between us, don't they?"

"It makes sense in my head. It's just that some days I wish I never woke up in that re-education room. Not death. Just...you know...back to the way things were before we found that old stone," she said, tears pouring down her cheeks and darkening her uniform in odd, uneven shapes. "Some days, I just want to leave this place."

"Don't you feel it, though? That burning in the chest? The glow tugging on us to keep moving? I don't know where this is headed, but I know it's the only way to get there," he said, swallowing the emotion in the back of his throat. "Crows, right?"

Joanna smacked her cheeks back and forth with each hand until she felt the emotion die down. Taking a deep breath, she pushed down on her friend's shoulder, hopped to her feet, then scuffled ahead of him to get a better look down the hall.

"Alright. Let's go. I've wasted enough time tonight," she said, rushing forward and staying below the window line. Heading toward the glow, Joanna turned left at the intersection with Heschel on her heels. Her heart skipped a beat seeing a light flash through the museum windows.

"Look at that!" said Heschel, covering his mouth after the outburst. "It's in the library. We're finally gonna make some real progress with Charlie's clue tonight."

Excitement had just begun to replace Joanna's anxiety when she reached for her device. Her eyes grew wide as she began digging through each of her pockets. She patted her grey jumpsuit up and down with nothing to show for it.

"Try your wrist," Heschel said with a smirk.

"Wrist? Yeah. That's right. I knew that," she said, wiping away the last few tears from the top of her cheeks. Pulling back her sleeve, she revealed her tablet and immediately began swiping windows and tapping on odd-named files. Heschel watched in amazement as she finally pulled up an old QR code—a black and white square made up of interconnected pixels. Quick Response codes were used by staff to secure doors all over the compound, including the museum, but this was an old code she stumbled upon in a shared folder on Stream. Neither of them knew if it was any good.

"It's green!" Joanna blurted out after nearly a dozen attempts at the scanner.

"Run to the back, quick," rushed Heschel. "I'll hold the handle so it doesn't snap shut so loud. GO!"

"What's the hurry?" Joanna asked.

"I hear footsteps down the hall. They'll be here any second."

Heschel eased the door shut before racing past the glow at the center of the large room. *Orb, I don't know your plan, but if you don't fizzle out, they're gonna come straight for us.* The orb vanished as soon as the thought left his mind, leaving them in the dark. Disoriented and not yet hidden, he tripped over Joanna, who happened to be hunkered down behind the administrator's desk. With a loud thud, his face hit the floor as a beam of light flashed across the room through the window beside the museum door he had just closed.

"How's your nose?" whispered Joanna.

Heschel shook his head. He could sense the monitor peering into the dark room, waiting for a sign of movement. After a few moments of absolute silence, another beam of light flashed across the room, followed by darkness, and finally, the sound of footsteps fading down the hall.

"Hesch, the glow's gone. I think I saw it dart between those bookshelves at the front of the room before I curled up."

"No, that's why I tripped over you," he said, pulling himself beside her. "All of a sudden it flashed to the right, behind that glass case with all the old computer gear in it. It flashed really bright and then vanished. I couldn't see anything after that...except for the ground."

As Heschel was describing the final movements of the glow, a strange rustling sound emanated from that direction. It was faint like a mouse might sound creeping along the edge of a kitchen floor at night. The two roommates froze. Joanna, staring into the shadows ahead, urged Heschel to investigate.

"Me? You want me to chase the creepy noise?" he said, tapping his chest and raising his eyebrows. The two silently argued, pointing, nudging, and rebuking.

"Alright, alright, alright," mouthed Heschel. "Let's check it out together. You go to the right through the Alphabet Coup memorabilia. I'll creep around to the left, past the ancient appliances. If something's back there, we'll corner it. Let's hope the glow hasn't gone far."

"On the count of three," Joanna whispered, leaning toward the memorabilia. "One…"

"Two…" followed Heschel, taking one step forward with a deep breath.

"Three," they said in unison, rushing down their dark paths.

The rustling escalated between them when out of the shadows, they heard, "Please don't hurt me!"

Heschel and Joanna stopped dead as two arms shot up from behind the case, followed by the silhouette of a head, then shoulders, and finally the lanky frame of a tall human.

10 Partners

"Chih?" Heschel choked out. "Is that…Is that you?"

"He…He…Hesch?" he stammered. "Joanna?" Chihming dropped his arms like bricks, took a deep breath, then plopped into the worn, plastic chair next to him. Grunting and sighing, he worked his way through a full body stretch before finally blurting out, "What on the edge are you two doing here? Is it really you? I mean, after that creepy event in the courtyard and the re-education, do you even remember anything?"

"We could ask you the same thing, Ming," shot Joanna, annoyed from the shock and tense from the stress of the passing patrol.

"It's good to see you, Chih," said Heschel. "I'm sorry I never reconnected with you about that Charlie comment. I've been distracted lately. But what are you doing here this late?"

"Me? I'm here every night," said Chih-ming, as though it were normal for a student to be outside their flat after lights out.

Hesch pulled out an empty chair across from Chih-ming and cautiously sat down. Joanna took a deep breath, relaxed her shoulders, then joined the others at the desk. "Was that patrol on the hunt for you or us?"

"I guess I don't know. They've never paused with a searchlight before," Chih replied.

"So what were you gonna tell me about Charlie that day? Have you been recruited to keep an eye on us too?" said Heschel, channeling his best, most professional Charlie imitation.

"Like a spy? No! Sheesh! It's just that…well…I don't know where to begin. How do I explain a weird light, and this burning, and what's the deal with that secret hole in your wall," he stammered, beginning to sweat. Chih-ming was tall for his age. At over six feet, he was a head above Heschel and towered over Joanna, though his anxious demeanor made him appear younger and smaller.

Heschel patted his friend on the shoulder. Chih-ming flinched. After all, physical contact wasn't normal. Heschel caught himself, rubbed his hands together, and carried on. "If you've seen the glow and know about the compartment, it sounds like you're in just as deep as we are. Besides, it was the glow that led us here tonight."

"Hesch," cut in Joanna, "do you really think Chih knows about the glow? I mean, personally? No offense, Ming, but from what I hear, a lot of students saw whatever happened in that courtyard. Don't forget what happened to Charlie when we let our guard down."

His eyes flashed at Joanna. Not anger, but sadness at the memory.

"Charlie…" mumbled Chih-ming, nodding his head as though agreeing with himself. "Listen, I gotta know. How were you two connected to Charlie? Was he the spy you're talking about?"

"Charlie was…a mentor of mine who…uh…was offering special Wide Awake training," said Hesch, realizing he wasn't quite ready to share all of their exploits' deep and deadly details.

Joanna, noticing Hesch stumble into a lie, interjected, "Yeah, like a student ambassador, you know…before they…uh…before he was transferred from the compound." Joanna's words faded to a whisper.

After an awkward moment of silence, Chih-ming said, "I'm not sure what's going on here, but I'm not an idiot. Are you really trying to tell me that Charlie was just an innocent WAFE who happened to get transferred from the compound soon after he and I translated the first relic from Greek to English right where you and I are sitting?"

Joanna and Hesch shifted in their seats. Their shock at the news told Chih everything he needed to know. Leaning back with his confidence rebounding, he said, "To be honest, ever since you two disappeared that whole week last month, I've been trying to connect the dots." Reaching into his pocket, he pulled out a dark, odd-shaped object and a couple of scraps of paper. For a moment he looked them over, wondering if he was doing the right thing. Convinced that he was, he set them on the table.

"Chih! This is the relic we buried on the edge!" said Heschel, jumping to his feet. "It was buried beneath the Creeping pine. How did you... You said you weren't spying on us!"

Shocked by Heschel's thunderous response, Chih reflexively snatched a scrap of paper back up from the table. Shielding his face with his left arm as though waiting to be struck, he blindly thrust the note toward Heschel, shouting, "It was you! You told me! Read it!"

Joanna sat back in her chair, clearly surprised by both Chih's claim and Heschel's reaction. She had spent enough time with Hesch to know that, though timid at times, he was as self-controlled as any student could be. It's why he had been identified as a Wide Awake. It's why she continued to believe they were on the right side of history in all this deceit. And this emotionally charged outburst seemed to come out of nowhere.

Heschel raised his hands and stepped back from the desk. *That wasn't cool. What am I doing? I've got to get a handle on these unexpected twists.*

"Whoa! Did I just hear your thoughts? You didn't move your mouth," stammered Chih.

Joanna patted him on the shoulder. She knew exactly how weird it was. After several deep breaths, Hesch took the note from Chih's hand, read it nice and slow, then calmly sat back down. After a few very long seconds, he handed the scrap to Joanna. Her wrinkled brow and wide-eyed surprise affirmed Heschel's bewilderment.

"You know, when I came out of that chemically-induced re-education coma, I was as clear-minded as I'd ever been in my life," Heschel said in a low, gruff voice. "I envisioned things I'd never thought of before. Stories from my past. Events zoomed in and with such focus that I thought I'd be able to put all the pieces of this mystery together without a hitch."

Joanna set the note down on the table. Chih had lowered his arms and was staring at the floor. She reached over, pat his forearm, and with a smile, said, "Well, Hesch, I'd say your handwriting could use a little work."

"Handwriting? I don't even remember writing this! I don't remember details from the chaos in the courtyard a few weeks ago. I need help...*we* need help figuring out what to do next," Hesch said, looking at Joanna, apologizing with his expression.

"Hesch, we've needed help from the beginning," Joanna said, her voice shaking as it rose in volume. "I mean, we didn't start this, did we? We saw that soft yellow light radiating from that hidden compartment all those months ago. We followed the clues. We followed the glow! It's the glow that's been helping us. It's the glow that's been guiding us. All of us! It's the glow that's rescued us from that barbaric brainwashing in The Adavis Center for Perversion! And the glow, whatever it is, will connect all the dots for us from here on out."

"It was the glow that first clued me in on the ancient language Charlie and I researched. And it was the glow that literally tugged and guided and even spoke to me in your room that night," said Chih-ming before tapping on the keyboard in front of him. The bright glow of a computer screen embedded in the glass table filled the room. Their shadows cast large on the walls behind them. Without another word, he quickly navigated through the back end of the Anti-Libertas library catalog. He moved so fast that neither Heschel nor Joanna could keep track of what links he clicked or which pages he scrolled through.

"Here it is," said Chih-ming, pointing to what appeared to be a line of code on a ledger of transactions neatly organized on the Anti-Libertas blockchain. Data that wasn't necessarily hidden from the students, though, not specifically made available to them either. Chih-ming had a way of maneuvering through the system like an experienced explorer with a compass in the wilds.

"What are we looking at, Ming?" asked Heschel. "I mean, it's obviously a log of all of Compound 40's communications, but what's so strange about that one line?"

"Read the title," said Chih-ming, spreading his fingers across the screen to zoom in on the text.

Heschel gasped at what he saw. Grabbing hold of Joanna's arm, he squeezed in amazement.

"Are you serious, Chih?" he whispered.

"Wait, some of those symbols are on the tablet," Joanna whispered back, her voice trembling with excitement.

"Not just the same symbols, but the very same heading. I interspersed them with English words just in case anyone around here happened to review the ledger," said Chih, smiling at his cleverness. "I know what it says." Clicking on the transaction link, he scrolled down to reveal his notes. "With the help of some old Middle Eastern stellas, parchments, and blocked internet translators, Charlie and I were able to figure out the first half of the tablet. I spent the last few weeks on the tablet I dug up finishing what we started. One symbol at a time. One word at a time. When it was safe, anyhow."

"Well, can we read it?" asked Joanna.

"I memorized it," said Chih. "I can't get it out of my head. It seems to sit on my chest too," he said, pointing straight toward his heart.

"Well?" said Heschel.

"It's from somebody named John. They said, 'If you love me, you will obey what I command. And I will ask the Father, and he will give you another Counselor to be with you forever—the Spirit of truth. The world cannot accept him, because it neither sees him nor knows him.'"

"*Father, counselor, spirit…*what do we do with this?" asked Hesch, speaking more to himself than the others.

"I'd hoped you would know. There are a lot of weird words in there, aren't there? *Love* and *father*. What's that all about? We had read about the unscientific notion of love as seekers, didn't we?" replied Chih, holding his chest. "All emotion and preference and hope."

"Is that everything?" asked Hesch, frustration growing in his voice. "Any highlighted words or letters or symbols? You know, like a cipher or a legend? A key? Anything? Tell me Charlie didn't die for a useless quote!"

"Hush!" Joanna snapped, jumping to her feet like a lioness. "Did you two hear that?"

11 The Huntress

"They're in the hall," Joanna whispered before dropping to the floor and crawling behind the narrow end of a display case filled with curated relics.

"Sure doesn't sound like a casual patrol," said Heschel.

"And they're early," Chih-ming observed. "It hasn't been more than ten minutes since that light flashed through the room."

"You remembered to replace the card in your device tonight, didn't you?" asked Joanna.

Heschel nodded, eyes wide and glued to the shadows beginning to float along the wall across from the museum's entrance. "Absolutely. I left it in the room. We should be invisible."

"They didn't trace me," said Chih. "I'm here all the time. I use a coded replacement when I'm out. Besides, mine's on the charging stand in my room. I even have a dummy device on the stand, plugged in just in case the flat is canvassed while I'm gone."

Joanna held her hand palm out toward the others for several seconds before quickly motioning downward. The universal sign for *Quiet! Get down!* Each student crouched a bit lower as the lock beeped, flashing a green LED before the heavy door crept open without a sound. In the center of the doorway appeared the silhouette of an armed monitor front and center with another by their side.

"I'm just relaying what I saw, lieutenant," said the supporting monitor staring at the device on their forearm. They were carrying a strange-looking camera mounted upright over their right shoulder on a gooseneck stand. "There was an unexplainable heat source coming from this room on my patrol less than fifteen minutes ago."

"And what did you find after inspecting the area?" asked Lieutenant Kresreb, her white hair aglow in the dim light of the safety sconces on either side of the doorway now activated with the proper door key. "You did investigate before calling for my assistance, didn't you?"

"What did I find?" echoed the monitor with a soft-spoken quivering voice.

"No doubt you did everything within your power to uncover the source of this mystery before wasting my time." The lieutenant's unique accent grew thicker as her patience grew thin. "Computers? Machines? Wild animals? Students!"

"I...I...you see...it...it didn't...." The young monitor's voice trailed off with chattering teeth and trembling lips.

Throughout the tense exchange, all three students slowly shrank into unnaturally compact lumps of flesh huddled on the floor. Of course, they knew that security had been on high alert lately. However, Lieutenant Kresreb had become more than a monitor to be concerned about—she had morphed into a ferocious animal on the hunt. Her career and reputation had been compromised because of these two out of control Observers, and she had no intention of letting them get away with it.

Heschel and Joanna had sensed something familiar yet off-putting with the lieutenant. They had felt it immediately upon her arrival months ago, but now, having another chance to witness her in action, their stomachs justifiably began to knot with each harsh word and every unsettling inflection in her voice.

After a moment of silence and a demoralizing stare, Lieutenant Kresreb lifted her arm toward the open room as though graciously ushering her terrified assistant into the museum. Without so much as a word of warning, she swung her arm with a grunt, backhanding the cheek of the monitor and knocking them to the ground. The trooper hit the floor head-first, crushing the camera with their body weight and passing out cold. Horrified, the remaining band of monitors in the hall froze.

All three students broke into a cold sweat at the sudden burst of violence and thoughts of their inevitable capture. Joanna, curling up like a hedgehog, let out a faint gasp. The room grew silent.

"I will not allow this sort of amateur policing on my watch!" shouted Lieutenant Kresreb to the unresponsive body lying next to her. "Do you see this?" she screeched at her device to the monitors surveilling on dispatch. Holding her wrist in a cock-eyed position, Kresreb forced them into silence as they stared at their peer unconscious on the floor. "Do you see your fellow monitor? This is what happens when you break protocol. You will either be diligent in executing your duties," she said coldly, her voice lowering to a gruff whisper, "or you will be violently relieved of them. Do we understand one another?"

Lieutenant Kresreb canceled the live feed before the team on the other end could respond. Ready for action, she flipped on the lights without wincing the way an average human does when eyes are used to the dark. Taking two large strides into the room, she paused, listening beyond the sound of the buzzing lights like a panther lying in wait for the kill.

The students froze in terror. Joanna, seeing the awkward

positions of Heschel and Chih, nearly gave them all away as she pursed her lips, trying to contain an ill-timed laugh. Hesch lay flat on his stomach with arms and legs stretched out in cockeyed positions. He looked like he'd fallen from the top of Chagrin Center with a sudden splat. Chih-ming, extremely tall and lanky, sat with his back against the desk, his legs sprawled out straight across an aisle, and his torso half bent sideways like a doll without support. *We train for situations like this in case Deplorables attack, and this is how these two…these strong, smart Observers respond in a pinch? I wonder if the chemical makeup of a young male teenager under stress impacts his intelligence in different scenarios?* she thought, unable to control her wide smile, even as Lieutenant Kresreb prowled dangerously close.

"These tracking devices are a bit outdated, aren't they?" said the lieutenant, breaking through the silence to whoever might be listening. "So easy to remove cards and corrupt codes. Sure, thermal cameras, when they aren't smashed on the floor, are a step in the right direction, but there are things that even our best trainers aren't capable of teaching. For instance, I can sense the infestation within this room. It's in the air. A thick, uneasy sort of pressure. I feel it all the more in my chest since that day in the courtyard. Something pulling me right here…right now."

Lieutenant Kresreb slipped deeper into the room like a snake in the yard, peering down dimly lit aisles. Her boots clapped ever-so-gently on the linoleum floor. Just loud enough for the disobedient students to keep tabs on her whereabouts.

The museum wasn't huge, but it was a labyrinth of artifacts, cases, desks, and displays. A person could spy the entire room from the right perch while remaining relatively hidden. The students, however, were not in the right position and had begun to dread their unavoidable arrest—a trip to The Adavis Center for Progress that would set them back several more weeks. What's worse is that it would place them directly into the terrifying hands of the new lieutenant now on the hunt.

Daring to look up from her cocoon, Joanna motioned for Heschel's attention. With as little force as possible, she began to stagger her breathing in an unnatural cadence. Inhale twice. Exhale three short bursts. Breathe in twice. Breathe out one long, slow breath.

Heschel, distracted by her distinctly out-of-whack breathing, peered in her direction with eyes questioning her sanity. *Seriously? We're on a secret mission with murderous guards hunting us, and this breathing exercise is how you choose to calm yourself down?*

"The glow," she mouthed. The spit from her tongue hitting the roof of her mouth seemed to be amplified in the silent room.

Heschel shook his head, his eyes softened. He knew what she was asking and had no way of producing. "You know I don't control it," he mouthed helplessly.

Immediately down the hall, the sound of half a dozen more monitors jogging towards them broke the tension of the hunt. Their steps came to a complete stop at the entrance to the museum, where several monitors were tending to their unresponsive compatriot.

"Lieutenant?" called a deputized monitor from the doorway. Their firm voice masked their fear of the white-haired leader lurking silently throughout the museum. "Lieutenant Kresreb! Principal Chicanery would like a word with you at Chagrin Center. Immediately."

Stepping out from behind a bookshelf directly to the left of the emboldened monitor, Lieutenant Kresreb appeared like a ghost with an unsettling snarl. "No need to raise your voice, sergeant," she whispered. "I'm right here, doing that one's job." Pointing to the limp monitor being placed on a stretcher, the lieutenant confidently stepped past the squad huddled around the doorway and over the body lying on the floor.

With a few barked orders, some loud shuffling, and the sound of the museum door closing firmly, the terrifying moment came to a sudden end. The students had managed to avoid arrest. At least for another fifteen minutes before the next scheduled patrol.

"That was a close one," said Heschel, rising to his feet, shaking his stiff arms, and wiggling his sleeping legs. "Did you notice her voice?"

"Yeah, I did," Joanna replied, unable to pinpoint why it sounded familiar.

"Am I missing something here?" Chih-ming chimed in. "They knew we were in here. They're hunting us! And you two are thinking about a voice? First of all, what's a *her*? And what's with that *love* and *father* language on the tablet? It reads like the ancient poetry we learned about as Seekers. It doesn't make sense, yet I can't stop thinking about it. Seems connected to this super uncomfortable feeling in my chest. Like it's burning off the pressure that's always been there. Like somehow it's all gonna work out. Charlie didn't tell me much of anything, so I don't know what I don't know, and I'm not so sure that I ought to know, but I think I want to know. You know?"

Heshel and Joanna locked eyes, smiled, then slowly turned toward their friend towering above them with arms raised and hands resting on his head, clenching his stark black hair like a mad scientist.

"You're right," said Heschel after a bit of silence. "We absolutely don't know what we don't know. But you do, Chih. You know more than you think. You know as much as we do now, and the glow is obviously connecting with you as much as either of us. But I think we need to spend a week laying low. They're getting too close. How about we just act like every other student at C-40 for a bit?"

Joanna, studying the unsettled expression on their new partner's face, agreed. "It's late, I'm worn out, and I don't think Kresreb will take it easy on us a second time."

Heschel reached out to give Chih a fist bump but turned away when he caught a glimpse of the second scrap of paper nearby. "It must have fallen on the floor in the commotion," he said, snagging it up and holding it close. "It's a sketch. It's another clue. The key! Joanna, do you remember the pews in Chagrin Center!"

 # 12 Back to Not-So-Normal

The next several days rolled by uneventfully. Joanna was enjoying the change of pace. It felt good to live the rhythm of an ordinary Observer again, even if it was only pretending. Deep down, though, she couldn't shake the supernatural attachment to the grander story of life beyond Compound 40—a story that remained a gigantic mystery.

"Have you noticed the lack of security lately?" asked Heschel, catching up to Joanna on their way to the cafeteria.

"Lack of...No! I've been enjoying normal student life for the time being," she said, continuing her steady stride into the courtyard.

"Don't you think it's strange that Kresreb and her band

of deputized monitors aren't hovering over us? That they aren't peeking around every corner or patrolling at the entrance to every class?" he wondered, his voice squeaking as he spoke fast.

"You said act normal. We all agreed to act normal for a week or so after the other night in the museum, didn't we? Well…this is me acting normal!" Joanna left Heschel behind while waving to some fellow Observers across the main path. Turning back, she added, "I'll save you a seat inside if you think you can handle a dose of compound routine for a day or two."

Heschel stopped, nervously laughed, then silently watched a flock of birds overhead as they returned from their winter getaway. After several minutes of gazing upwards into the stark blue sky, he grew unsettled, shook the clouds from his mind, then looked around in search of a spying eye. Nothing. As it turned out, he was standing in the very same place where the glow had revealed itself to the Kresreb. Which also happened to be the same place he and Joanna stood the previous fall discussing crows and murders before following the white-haired elder, who he now knew was the lieutenant, into Chagrin Center for their hearing.

The sun was shining and warm. He wanted to take Joanna's challenge and experience a low-key, back-to-normal week as a student, just as they had agreed, but since this all began, normal hadn't returned. He walked around the invisible circle where the monitors had fallen. Shuffling his way to where Leuitenant Kresreb had been, he paused before strolling over to where he had been pushed down. His chest immediately began to burn. He could hear his heartbeat thumping in his ears, and his hands began to tingle. Like a dream or a vision, the event began replaying right before his eyes. He knew it happened, of course he did. After that re-education fail, it all seemed crystal clear. But now, watching it play out again, he couldn't believe his eyes. *It really, truly happened.* But it was more than that. Details he couldn't have known at the time were revealed. It was as if he were managing a 360-degree holographic view of the event. He was speeding it up, slowing it down, and zooming in on the things he hadn't seen.

Look at that! The orb hadn't gone rogue. It wasn't out of control or anything like that. I was guiding it. No! We... were working together. It guided my thoughts, keeping my anger and confusion in check. And look at my hands! I released it! I directed it!

Heschel walked around the circle again, navigating the scene with cupped hands. As though holding an invisible ball, when he rotated his hands in one direction, the scene moved forward. When he wanted to see something again, in more detail, he would rotate his hands the opposite way, and the scene would rewind faster or slower with the slightest hand gesture carrying him from one moment to the next. What's more, he couldn't see anything either before or after the altercation. It was as if the glow had only given him permission to see what it wanted him to see.

The courtyard was barren as lunch was being served and afternoon sessions were starting. On his final lap around the circle, he paused beside the orb at the center. *Strange how it stopped mid-glide. It's like it changed its mind.* He stood behind the orb with a translucent Lieutenant Kresreb directly across from him—the orb in between them. *It was returning to me, but I stopped it. I changed its course. I wanted Kresreb to leave us alone. I...I wanted her out of the picture. Joanna's right. I have more control than I realize.*

 # 13 Normal Has Left the Compound

"**W**ell, if it isn't the infamous young Observer, Heschel, here in the flesh," said Principal Chicanery standing within the main entrance. He was greeting students on their way to the cafeteria. Though it wasn't abnormal for him to do this, he hadn't been spending as much time among the student population since the re-education catastrophe. Heschel nodded, reaching out to shake the principal's hand. "Strange natural events happening lately. No doubt, as a WAFE, you're all the more connected to Compound 40's most extraordinary activities," he continued, ignoring Heschel's polite greeting.

Heschel knew how intertwined Principal Chicanery

was with the chaos in the shadows. They both knew. And they both knew they both knew. It had become a deeply personal game to the czar of C-40. A game he had grown accustomed to winning over the last several decades as he amassed control within The Chamber. But now, Chicanery's blatant acknowledgment of the game in public emboldened Heschel to respond. To abandon ordinary altogether.

"You've seen the glow before," said Heschel, his eyes sharp and steady on the snake in front of him. "It scares you, doesn't it?"

"Heschel? What happened to blending in until things cool down?" he asked with a smile twice as big as usual and twice as unsettling. "I'm simply referring to my updates on Stream. I work hard at sending the right message at just the right time. To ease fears, you know? I don't doubt that you and your small band of adventurers keep tabs on these sorts of things. For instance, that ball lightning in the courtyard last month is still a hot topic among the students. And those light tremors happening more frequently have got to be a bit disorienting—particularly for a student who has already been through so much, you know, with that mislabeled IV in the infirmary and all."

Principal Chicanery's tone was just as it always was, professional and almost warm. But this new phase of openly discussing the secrets he had worked so hard to stamp out unnerved him. Deciding it was time to go, Heschel began to step back when someone blocked his path.

"Chicanery, these unacceptable events have unnerved my squad. They're paranoid! Now hearing and seeing strange sights and sounds all over the compound at all hours of the night," barked Lieutenant Kresreb, who had been lurking in the shadows across from Chicanery and now stood immediately behind her prey.

"You were there that night, the member of The Chamber who greeted us at the door," said Heschel, turning to face the infamous huntress. "The one who travels from one compound to the next taking care of…issues. The one I'm not supposed to remember. You're here to end what Chicanery can't control, aren't you? But even you, the mighty Lieutenant Berserk, that's what they called you at the other compounds, right? Even you can't control it!"

Lieutenant Kresreb froze. Her eyes began to blink uncontrollably. Her head began to twitch. For a moment, no more than a flash, Heschel thought he saw something like a burning ember deep within the pupils of her eyes. It was the orb only different, like a dying fire within her mind, or maybe a rekindling. Whatever it was, Heschel dropped his guard when he saw it. That's when the huntress struck.

Like a big cat, her paw shot forward, striking her target's throat. Her grip was firm. Heschel was immediately reminded of his youth and inexperience. He knew this trained executioner could bring him to an end without so much as breaking a sweat right then and there.

Her stare, however, terrified Heschel the most. A moment

before, he glimpsed an ember glowing deep within her eyes, but now her eyes were cold and pale, empty black pupils. Where Principal Chicanery managed to embody civility in his rage, the lieutenant seemed to have abandoned her conscience.

"You're nothing more than Deplorable offspring," she growled. "And you know what we do with little boys who…."

"That's enough, lieutenant!" cut in Chicanery. "ENOUGH!"

Once again, Principal Chicanery impatiently dismissed the white-haired, ill-tempered leader, just as he had done during that initial interrogation after the fall Sojourn. Lieutenant Kresreb released her grip. Fumbling over her chest pockets, she angrily searched for the pins and badges that typically adorned her elite suit. Realizing that she was still in costume, wearing the standard-issue jumpsuit that all lieutenants wear, her cheeks flushed with rage before storming into the courtyard.

Without another word, Principal Chicanery nodded and then headed upstairs to his office. Heschel stood motionless, his stomach caught up in his throat.

"Oh! Heschel," said Chicanery, stopping a dozen feet away. "I'm heading to the infirmary later to prepare for a meeting with a special guest. You seem a bit under the weather. Care to join? I'm sure Dr. Breach, who, sadly, recently departed to serve another compound, left something lying around that could help with your emotional disposition."

Chicanery smiled, shook his head, then carried on his way.

 ## 14 Change of Plans

"**I** was beginning to worry," said Joanna, her cheeks flushed. Without looking up, she continued to dissect safe pieces of vitabread from the moldy slice on her tray. "I didn't mean to ditch you out in the courtyard. It's just that it's been a bit calm and quiet these last few days, and…."

"Listen, I get it. We've been…." Heschel began to say, trying to find a way to tell her about Chicanery, when she cut him off from his empathetic reply.

"I wasn't finished, Hesch," she noted with a tone that commanded attention. "I was saying that while it's been quiet, it's also been unsettling. I don't want to admit it, but it feels strange not seeking out more clues. And it's impossible to stop thinking about the glow."

"There's a sort of peace in being caught up in its illumination," he replied under his breath as if speaking to himself.

"Before all this began, I hadn't thought about guidance or protection or truth. The Chamber took care of all that, and we were just, you know, clueless robots or something. I didn't have to think about trust because I didn't know we could respond a different way," she said, slowly shoving moldy bits of vitabread into her carryall again. "But we've uncovered a different way, and I prefer choosing to trust each other over mindless obedience. It feels warmer."

Heschel was just about to agree when Chih-ming wandered into the cafeteria.

"Chih?" said Hesch, waving to grab his friend's attention from across the room. "Chih, what are you doing here during second period lunch?"

"Yeah, it's a little strange," he said, nervously looking around while dropping into an open seat across from them. "Hey, Joanna. Yeah…well, it's weird, I think. I just got a message from my floor's WA that I should begin eating lunch during the first period. An order straight from the top."

When he finished speaking, both Chih and Joanna turned toward Heschel. They sat in silence, watching his face contort as if under pressure. His lips pursed then relaxed, smacking together over and over with a popping sound. They waited as his mind filtered through the random alteration in Chih-ming's schedule. Heschel couldn't recall a single instance where a student had been transferred mid-quarter like this. He and Joanna had been eating lunch with the same mix of Observers, Interpreters, and Appliers since they graduated from the Seeker class. So had Chih. No one joined, and no one left. Clearly, Principal Chicanery had something devious in mind. Something destructive.

"Chicanery's up to something," whispered Hesch, leaning over the table and motioning the others to do the same. "I just ran into him in the hall. He's not the same stoic leader he's always been. Something's off. The same with Kresreb. She's cracking. Look, I think we need to move quickly. I was wrong about playing it normal. We've got to dive in tonight."

"So we're officially done with regulation and routine?" asked Joanna with a smirk.

"Normal?" Chih muttered, choking on a chunk of vitabread. "I chased an orange ball of light down a hall into your flat. I watched a door open and close on its own. I've been pushed and pulled and…."

"And now it's time to figure out what this tablet's all about, don't you think?" said Heschel, wiping wet bread crumbs from his forehead after Chih's outburst. "Tonight, we'll meet between the ferns on the west side of Chagrin Center. Joanna and I will bring the tablets, the note with the pew sketch on it, and some pencils. Chih, you bring that passage. You still remember it, right?”

“I can’t stop repeating it.”

“Tonight. Two a.m. Make sure Lieutenant Kresreb and her minions aren’t tailing you, Chih. We’ll do the same. If the glow appears, trust it. It’s proven itself inside and out.”

 ## 15 Crows in the Nest

The moment their devices flashed two o'clock, the glow joined the fray. Though in two different rooms, on two separate floors, all three students experienced the same supernatural events in the same way. First a burning in the chest. Deep and sharp. It started on the skin, like an insect bite, then sunk deeper like a knife into the muscle. But it wasn't just physical. Their insides twisted up with the kind of excitement that comes at the start of a new adventure. Exciting yet scary.

Heschel and Joanna had gathered their supplies immediately following light's out. Joanna's carryall had become a necessity, though few students beyond Seeker carried them. She had forgotten to empty that day's vitabread stash from the main pocket, which made Heschel jump when he felt the soft, furry, mouse-like object inside as he began to stuff it with the two notes, extra scraps of paper, a few stubby, well-used pencils from their secret cubby, a small spindle of twine, a lighter, and the USB drive—a bundle of items they had learned might help in a pinch. Joanna's furious laugh at Heschel's faux-rodent panic eased their growing anxiety. They decided to split the tablet pieces between them, just in case.

Having recited the secret passage to himself more times than he could count, Chih managed to fall asleep. Unlike his two friends, Chih's flatmate was very much a student embedded in the Anti-Libertas worldview. It wasn't their fault, after all, Chih had been that way until recently too. It simply meant that he didn't have the freedom to pace and prepare. Instead, he slept. And he slept well. At two a.m. on the dot a burning in his chest stirred him to his feet like a startled dog ready to chase a squirrel.

At approximately 2:01, all three students left their rooms. Silently creeping across the compound, Chih managed to take the lead, beating Heschel and Joanna to the west side of Chagrin Center. He had maneuvered this midnight run more than any other student. While he was sure he could manage it blindfolded, this particular route along the western side was new. Though he hadn't yet seen the orb, the warmth in his chest reassured him that the glow, whatever it was, was with him every step of the way.

"Wow! These ferns are enormous!" said Chih as the others arrived. "I remember planting these when we super-young Seekers. Landscaping duty. I haven't paid any attention to them since."

"Anyone see anything out there? Monitors? Kresreb? Eyes in the sky tracking you?" asked Hesch, looking through the lush ferns and across the circle. "I haven't seen anything abnormal. And the cameras seem to be fixed in place, which is pretty normal too, I guess. Maybe too normal, if you know what I mean?"

As Joanna distributed the supplies, each one immediately practiced writing random letters on their scrap of paper. They all *knew* how to write. They had learned the skill in their introductory design sessions when they were Seekers. But it felt strange, like going back in time and marking cave walls or drawing with sticks in the sand.

Hesch cleared his throat for attention and then quickly followed up with the gameplan after they entered the chamber. They would have one hour to record as many Greek symbols and corresponding numbers as they could manage. Beginning with the pews to the right of the stage, the dead-center of twelve concentric circles of benches divided up into seven sections, each would cover a complete area before working their way to the right—one section at a time. Of course, they agreed to pause every fifteen minutes, roll beneath the nearest pew, and wait for the patrolling monitor to pass. If all went according to plan, they would be back in their flats and fast asleep by 3:30 a.m.

The building was dark, and the halls were cold. Fear creapt in as they navigated the stone passageways until a faint light appeared just above Heschel's head. It started small, about the size of an acorn. Its glow pulsed like a dimming flashlight. Yet, within thirty seconds or so, it increased to about the size of a bowling ball and was far too bright to stare at.

"Hesch, are you doing that?" Joanna asked.

"I'm not sure," he whispered, continuing to creep forward along the wall. "It sounds strange, but I had just begun to think how encouraging it would be for all of us to see the glow right about now. Seriously! The idea had just popped into my mind when I felt the burning in my chest begin to rise. That's when a flicker of light lit up the hall… and…well, you know."

"We're here," said Chih as they arrived at a set of wooden double doors, each with a small window about face level with Hesch. "It looks clear in there, but I think we ought to save talking for emergencies only."

Chih was steadily pushing the right side open when the hinges began to squeak loud and drawn out like an embarrassing stomach growl at the start of a test in a session full of students. Even the glow seemed to falter at the sound. Joanna, the last in line, pushed the others through the door, forced it closed, then covered their mouths with her hands while listening for movement in the halls. Nothing happened. As soon as she released her grip, the glow, still hovering over Heschel, shot into the air above them, split into three orbs, then descended upon the right shoulder of each student. Chih stood taller. Joanna breathed deeper. Heschel closed his eyes, imagined the mission at hand, then winked at his friends with a subtle smile. Pencils and papers in hand, they nodded and set to work.

The first fifteen minutes went by without much flare. Heschel had already moved on to another section when his alarm sounded. Like clockwork, all three hid as a clueless monitor pushed open a door on the opposite side of the hall. Flashing their light haphazardly across random rows, they appeared disinterested in their post. The students laid still with ears so attuned to the silence that they could hear the monitor's relaxed breathing. Without so much as a flicker, the orbs continued to illuminate the darkness around each student. At the same time, the monitor, utterly oblivious to the light, took a deep breath, mumbled something about "those rancid Deplorables," then backed out of the great hall without setting even one foot inside.

"Pssst. Hey, you two. Are you finding what I'm finding?" asked Heschel in a coarse whisper as soon as the door closed.

"I don't know," Chih replied, "but does anyone know

how many words we're looking for? I've only found one so far, and it's numbered seven on the pew, which is weird."

"Why is that weird?" Joanna asked. "The pews are numbered in order. There's nothing all that mysterious about it."

"No, not the order of the pews," Chih replied, snatching up a handful of his dark hair. "It's just that the word on the pew isn't the seventh word in the passage. It's…It's… It's not *supposed* to be in order!" As soon as he'd blurted it out, his face tingled with a static buzz as his eyes began to glow. Not like a cat's eyes at night in reflection, but an internal sort of glow, a bioluminescent effect. It was subtle but unmistakable as Heschel and Joanna watched in awe. The deeper he thought about the mystery, the brighter his eyes grew. "The words on the pews have been intentionally mixed up, and the numbers they're correlated with are their assigned position in the key. That's it! Check every pew. There'll be twelve, maybe eighteen if these are what I think they are."

"I've got three," called out Heschel.

"Two," Joanna followed. "We've got a long way to go. Let's cover the balcony together last."

"Wait!" Chih nearly shouted with excitement, his mind racing as his eyes darted back and forth across the hall. "I'm not sure how to explain it...but…but I think I know where to look for the rest. It's like the wormwood symbols are glowing an eerie greenish hue. Can't you see it? Like certain pews are radiating a signal. That one to your right, Joanna! And that one, two rows back from you, Hesch!"

Between the following three security alarms, cheers with each discovery, and the random "Doh!" after thumping a shin or an elbow against a bench, time flew by as they made their way to the balcony for the remaining clues. Just after the last alarm had sounded, they were on the uppermost right side of the balcony, the darkest point in the entire hall, when a door on the main floor swung open. Deputized monitors hastily marching single file behind Lieutenant Kresreb fell in line across the red and black granite Anti-Libertas logo at the center of the hall. Facing the empty stage, they stood at attention.

 **16 Not-So-Secret Meeting**

"**A**TTENTION!" commanded Lieutenant Kresreb.

"Bring them in," said Principal Chicanery, casually entering the hall from the rear of the stage. Making his way up to the podium—his podium—The Chamber entered closely behind, pausing at their respective positions across the stage while mocking the theatrics of the midnight hearing.

"Enough bickering!" Chicanery shouted, casting a nasty stare at the elite group sharing the stage with him. "You don't think I'm in control of my actions? Of my compound? And yes, this *is* my compound!"

From the hushed troop at the foot of the stage, Lieutenant

Kresreb cleared her throat. While Kresreb didn't recall her quarrel with Chicanery the previous fall on that stage, she wasn't about to waste any more time on what she thought was a ridiculous hearing. If she'd had her way, the Deplorable would already be fish food over the falls floating facefirst downstream.

"Yes, Kresreb?" asked Chicanery, slowly shifting his focus from the obtuse leadership to this annoying thorn in his side. "Why doesn't it surprise me that you feel the need to say something as though I haven't already heard everything you have to say?"

"Principal," she started with an out-of-place sweetness, "don't you think it would be a better use of my time, ahem, our time, during this fly-by-night tribunal if you were to avoid these petty arguments better left to boardrooms with your corrupted Chamber-pot?"

Chicanery smiled, lowered his eyes toward the logo beneath her feet, then shook his head while letting out a deep and terrifying belly laugh.

"Did you see that?" asked Joanna, barely whispering.

"You mean the flickering lights as he laughed?" said Heschel. "Yeah. I feel something building. Like static electricity filling the room. Don't you?"

"For sure. I can smell it too. Like hot solder," added Chih.

"Principal Chicanery told me about tonight," said Hesch.

"He said he had a meeting. I assumed it would have already happened, ya know, during normal hours and in an office or something. I didn't think much of it other than that we needed to move fast, but now that we're here, caught up in the shady meeting, I think we're supposed to witness what's coming. I think the glow wanted us here tonight."

No sooner had Heschel finished speaking when the door at the far right side of the hall swung open, making a loud crack as it smashed into the block wall behind it. A muffled shouting followed as three people entered the hall. The first person to enter appeared too disheveled to be a member of Compound 40.

From their terrible point of view beneath the pews high up on the balcony and with the lights dim and flickering throughout the hall, it looked like a cloth bag was covering the individual's head. The young Observers could only guess that some unknown person from some strange place was in some serious trouble.

Two deputized monitors immediately entered with their shock rifles pressed into the prisoner's back. The mysterious wild man continued to shout unintelligible phrases as the two unphased guards shoved them forward. With each blind step, the person grew emboldened, as if they knew exactly where they were heading and had a message to share.

"They're freaking out, Hesch. We gotta do something," Joanna said, turning away from the commotion below.

Watching intently, Hesch had begun to crawl toward a better post. He sensed something stirring and wanted to be in a position to make fast and clear decisions. He wanted to be ready to follow the glow.

"Look at his walk," Heschel pointed out. "He's not scared at all. He's never been more confident. You can tell a lot about a person by how they walk. He looks like he owns the place. Like he's supposed to be here."

"You sound like you know who he is," said Chih.

"It's the man from the cafeteria. A Deplorable," said Heschel. "It's a secret hearing to convict him and…well… who knows what Kresreb will do with him afterward."

The contingent of monitors stood motionless while Chicanery continued his awkward laugh louder and harder, gasping for air and smacking the podium. Regaining control, he smiled at the sight of the Deplorable standing directly in front of him at the foot of the stage. The room was silent except for the faint growing buzz of the glow.

Chicanery's eyes locked onto the figure. His lips remained perfectly still as he spoke. *I know why you're here, you treasonous degenerate. And I know you can hear me right now, don't be a fool. It's embarrassing how you people of the light refuse to give up the dead ways of the past, secretly brainwashing our simple-minded Observers with hidden messages and magic.*

"I've broken no legitimate law. No civil law. No moral

law. And no divine law," said the man. His voice was as rough and authentic as his clothing. "I have no idea what you're babbling on about, Chicanery."

Kresreb stepped toward the prisoner. Looking up to Chicanery with piercing eyes full of anger and confusion, she asked, "What's going on here? You haven't made a sound yet…yet this dog is answering questions."

"Get back in line, you old, miserable failure of a woman!" In a spitting rage, Principal Chicanery unleashed on the lieutenant. "You have no honor! No respect! No ability to discern when to speak and when to shut your wrinkled mouth! It's why you're down there and I'm up here. It's why you're completely oblivious to the desperate groans of the old ways. It's why re-education works so easily on you time and again!"

Up on the balcony, Chih began to sniff around. "It smells like an electrical fire in here," he said as the lights flickered more dramatically. "Like it did last year, hours before that mysterious fire in the lecture hall."

Heschel, captivated by the action below, watched as Lieutenant Kresreb stepped back in shock, grabbing her chest as though in pain. In an instant, she looked old and weak—a shadow of the terrifying huntress stalking them since her arrival. Again, Chicanery smiled, clearly satisfied with Krereb's response. Without skipping a beat, he turned his attention back toward the Deplorable.

You will be terminated. You have nothing to offer us. You and your people had their chance years ago, before the war ended and your light was snuffed out. Chicanery stood tall with his shoulders back. The Chamber said nothing. Heard nothing. "Do you have anything to say that's worth hearing before your execution?"

I have something to say on his behalf. Rising as he interjected, Heschel matched the confident stance of the prisoner down below. *Whoever this man is, he isn't the one revealing the truth. You know what it is that's leading this…this reality check or whatever you want to call it. This rebellion. He's innocent. As innocent as Charlie was. As desperate as Maria.*

Chicanery growled as he and the Deplorable simultaneously looked upward into the dark corner of the empty balcony. Heschel stood unflinchingly with the glow hovering over his right shoulder, ablaze for all to see.

"Heschel!" shouted Chicanery, his voice cracking in disbelief.

Trained to respond with flight for their protection, the remaining members of The Chamber rushed to leave the stage. Pounding on the door, they demanded that monitors on the outside rescue them. It didn't budge. The monitors on the floor split in two. One squad headed for the stage to protect the elites. The other fanned across the floor in search of an unlocked exit and a route to the balcony. Like their Anti-Libertas leaders, they were trapped. The metallic smell began to permeate the room.

Chih, it's time to stand, said Heschel. *It's time to step into your namesake. To be the man who stands tall with purpose and power. The man your parents intended you to be.*

Joanna, we've been here before, encouraged Hesh, his inner voice gentle and inviting. *You and I, we've followed the glow to the edge and back. It's time to stop secretly following the light and let it shine through us, face to face.*

Ignored in the chaos unfolding, Kresreb fell to the ground convulsing in pain. Visions of her childhood, the war, her rise to power within the Alphabet Coup, the tortured faces of the students she had chemically and mentally experimented on, and the glow at work within during her most recent round of re-education. Laying on the cold granite floor, she imagined the light as it appeared in the courtyard. She saw it spare their lives. She gasped at the sight of Heschel controlling it. Immediately feeling the same burning in her chest that everyone who encountered the glow felt, Kresreb audaciously rose to her feet.

I agree with the young WAFE, she cut in, responding to Heschel, who flashed a look in her direction. After locking eyes, she turned her attention to the elder tyrant grasping for control. *You hypocrite! You abuse the power of the glow in one breath while denying it exists in another breath. It's time! No more lies, Chicanery. Like every other compound, C-40 is internally collapsing under the weight of your*

*bankrupt Anti-Libertas ideas. You're collapsing too...and
so am I. But I'm not done yet!*

 ## 17 Kresreb Goes Berserk

"**Y**ou're off the bloody edge!" howled Principal Chicanery as the lights in the room crackled with electrical overload before flashing out in a smoky haze. "Who do you think you are? I should never have listened to you—you blundering wreck of a woman so easily entranced by that ancient religion. You'll immediately detain those students if you have any loyalty left in your decrepit frame!"

Standing tall on a bench in the light of the glow, Heschel wasn't surprised by the divide growing within The Chamber. However, he wasn't sure what to make of the uncomfortable compassion welling up in his heart for the scrappy lieutenant. With his chest burning he knew he had to speak up or shut up. Finally, he called out, "This old woman set out to exterminate us. She deserves this humiliating rejection. I know she does! Yet I feel sorry for her. After all, if the glow hadn't infiltrated our minds, no doubt all three of us would be following in her footsteps. Hunting the disobedient in the name of inclusive unity."

Once again, he called his friends to join him in the light. This time, without hesitation, the two Observers confidently rose to join the courageous WAFE shoulder to shoulder. The orbs, the only light source in the hall, were now visible to everyone in the room. It was unlike anything most of them had ever seen—or could remember.

"Joanna, you still have the USB, right?" Heschel asked, keeping his eyes fixed on the tension below.

"Of course. It's right here," she said, patting the satchel attached to her side. Hesch nodded.

"Chih, I want you to take all our notes, sketches, everything we've discovered on the pews tonight," said Hesch. Pulling several scraps of paper from his pocket and folding them up, he handed them over. Motioning to Joanna to do the same, he said, "You know the passage, Chih. You know the symbols. You know the chain. Now it's time to connect the dots for us."

Chih-ming nodded obediently.

"As for me, I'll hold onto the stones," said Hesch, reaching toward Joanna to collect the half she had been keeping safe. "I feel we're not quite done with these just yet."

"Shouldn't we keep them apart? You know…for safety?" she asked, hesitant to agree.

"I think it's best if each of us carries a full piece of the puzzle," he pushed back. "To own it like our lives depend on it. You're already carrying the most important piece. The piece that Deplorable down there risked his life to get into our hands. Same goal. New plan. Okay?"

As soon as Joanna handed over the black stone fragment, the orbs spun off in a brilliant flash beyond the balcony. Much like the glow had done over the cliff during the Sojourn. This time, instead of disappearing, the orbs began to multiply. Not into smaller particles as though they were diminishing in power or presence but into equally impressive orbs ablaze with purpose. One after the other rapidly appearing and buzzing and swirling like a tornado of stars shining beneath the beautifully rebuilt glass dome.

"I've watched the footage, Chicanery," growled Kresreb. "You think something as explosive as the destruction of this great hall of justice can be wiped from the cloud? I watched that glow tease and tromp all over you. I have more backup files secured on the chain than you do brain cells. You're just an old farm boy out of his league. And you know what? You're not in charge anymore—can't you see that?"

Principal Chicanery and the remaining members of The Chamber stood in shock at Kresreb's emboldened disregard for authority as orbs began to surround her. Her actions were unheard of—a form of social-credit cannibalism the students had never witnessed before. The old huntress stood firmly at the center of the granite logo adorned by the humming and buzzing tornado of lights. The elites watched in disbelief as she morphed into a more youthful version of herself, now radiating with energy and eyes aglow.

"I don't have to explain myself to you, Kresreb!" Chicanery shouted, his voice drowned out by the static buzz of the glow. "I don't have to...."

The room went dead silent.

It was the sort of heavy silence that sparks an unbearable pressure. A strain that caused their eyes to water and their ears to ring in a pulsing rush of pain. The students reached out to anchor one another in place, wincing with every pulse. If monitors were moving—they didn't know. If Chicanery had escaped—they didn't care. The only thing they could think of was the intensifying pressure, each with a firm hope that it would end sooner than later. Of course, they knew it would end. They knew because the glow endlessly moved with purpose and always followed through.

Just as everyone seemed to reach their breaking point— the silence broke with a burst of light that sent shockwaves through the darkness. Orbs once swirling like a mini tropical storm around Kresreb scattered on mission to subdue every monitor, member of The Chamber, and even principal Chicanery himself. And Lieutenant Kresreb was at the center of it all, glowing an otherworldly glow, watching, and waiting to strike.

Moving like a wildebeest seeking revenge among a pack of hyenas, Kresreb, empowered by the glow with supernatural strength and agility, joined in the hunt for her newly marked prey. With the orbs beginning to detain the panicking deputized monitors, Kresreb went straight for the head of the pack. Leaping like a tiger from the floor to the stage, the huntress landed face to face with her abusive mentor.

Instinctively she grabbed Chicanery by the collar. Effortlessly she lifted the old warden from the wooden floor, tossing him against the wall several feet away. With a growl that wrenched the spines of the elites cowering next to her, Kresreb snatched them up one by one. Her petite arms squeezed the oxygen out of her victims' lungs one exhale at a time until their limp bodies were piled high alongside the unconscious monitors subdued by the glow. The young Observers hardly moved a muscle as they watched Krereb go berserk from their perch above. Meanwhile, Heschel kept an eye on the Deplorable passed out on the cold granite floor.

The pile of inert bodies slowly grew until Chicanery alone remained. It had become a standoff between the two most vicious dogs in the pack, yet it didn't seem to phase Chicanery that he was doomed. That the glow he had tried to stamp out, the glow that had empowered an ancient worldwide movement—this glow was now fully empowering one of the most dangerous and cruel Anti-Libertas adherents he had ever known. Yet he refused to accept defeat.

"Why doesn't he just give up?" asked Joanna, breaking the silence on the balcony.

"He can't. He believes his view of the world—his utopia here at Compound 40—can succeed. No matter how many times it's been tried, he's convinced that he alone carries the torch forward," whispered Heschel, struck by the apparent absurdity of the movement.

"He led the charge against that ancient system and knows it's possible to suppress it. He knows better than anyone," said Chih.

"And he's convinced he can do it again. Right here. Right now," Hesch agreed.

Kresreb had Chicanery cornered. His eyes scoured the room for options—from one door to the next, up to the students, and back down to the unconscious Deplorable he wished he had eliminated back in the hot spot. With a deep sigh, he kneeled, put his hands together the way so many Deplorables had done pleading and praying, then bowed his head to the ground like a pious monk in worship. Just as his forehead touched the floor, security lights above each exit flashed on, and the sound of magnetic door locks clicked in release. The glow had finished its work. It had awakened the mind of the most wickedly progressive member of The Chamber at just the right time. Then, having completed its work, it vanished. The tornado of lights dissipated, and the burning in the young Observers' chests flared up again.

It's time for the three of you to finish your mission, said Kresreb without moving a muscle. *You have what you need, don't you?*

I don't know what to say, offered Hesch. *How do we thank you? Where will you go? Does this mean you've officially abandoned The Chamber? That you've switched sides?*

This is bigger than sides. I've finally done something good and true and right with my life, she said. Turning back to look at the three of them, Kresreb paused with tears in her eyes at the sight of these brave young students covered in the ancient glow. *I remember watching my government strangle the glow in my hometown as a child. I didn't understand it. It scared me. All of it. The glow. The fighting. The fear. The confusion. My parents tried to explain something about a helper, an advocate given to those who believed...but I never understood it. It wasn't allowed. Even our schools, influenced by the growing Alphabet Coup, adopted anti-oikos regulations. Rules that pressured students to rat on parents who spoke against The*

Chamber. And those who did, like me, were rewarded. I was the most popular rat in my district. But I get it now. I finally see what my parents tried to pass on to me in secret.

It doesn't feel right just leaving you here…alone, replied Joanna, tears forming. *There are hundreds of monitors out there who won't rest until you're….*

Before Joanna could finish, Lieutenant Kresreb screeched a bone-chilling squeal of pain. "What are you waiting for?" the old huntress choked out. "Crows. CROWS!" she yelled, her final words echoing through the chamber.

"I agree!" growled a vengeful voice from behind the shocked lieutenant. Rising, he pushed the wounded, weak creature over. The meaty thump of her body collapsing onto the wooden stage made them cringe. "What are you waiting for, young murder? Isn't there someplace you ought to be flying off to right now?" mocked the principal as he wiped off his Old Timer pocket knife, folded it, then slipped it back into his chest pocket.

 **18 Now or Never**

Four of the doors on the main floor swung open with a bang. More monitors poured in than the students had ever seen in one location. They were angry and on a mission to rescue the principal and exterminate anyone or anything in their way. Each monitor robotically entered the room with caution raising their shock rifles in a sweeping motion before spreading out in a well-rehearsed offensive pattern. Knowing nothing of the glow, the secret meeting, the students' disobedience, or Lieutenant Kresreb's mutinous actions, these troops came in hot and ready.

"Hesch?" asked Chih, his voice shaking.

"Ming?" he replied.

"Do you still think we'll be in bed by 3:30?" he asked with a smirk, his lanky frame as shaky as his voice.

"She's right, you know?" Joanna cut in. "Crows. We're a growing murder of crows, and we'll stick together like one. It's not a game anymore. We're no longer just a few students breaking compound rules after dark. We're traitors…and.…"

"And we do exactly what Chicanery ordered us to do," said Heschel, leaping over the back of the pew and crouching on the floor. The others followed. As soon as they were out of sight, dozens of electrified shock darts whipped over their heads. Shock darts were about the size of a thumb with a snub nose needle on the tip of a rechargeable pack. A vital tool among Compound 40 security. Heschel, the only WAFE among his friends, had trained several times with low-power packs after becoming a WA and knew just how incapacitating they were.

"There's no turning back, you two," said Hesch, his eyes watering. His friends nodded, uneasy emotion welling up within them."

Chih-ming wiped his eyes. "So then…where to?"

Hesch had already thought up a plan. More and more, the orb was preemptively impacting his natural processes, like a booster into his bloodstream. Their relationship had surpassed acquaintance, entangled in a deeper sort of otherworldly partnership. The plan? They needed a decoy.

It was time for them to put more skin in the game—to let the light shine through their wild actions.

"When we exit the balcony through the rear door, you two are gonna make a run for the museum. Are we clear?" asked the young leader, dressing up his attitude with as much Charlie as he could muster. "I know what you wanna say, Joanna. Here's the deal—we each have our piece of the puzzle to protect. Each of us is vital, but they're gonna want to take out the leader first. I guess that's me. You two unlock the message, I'll get there as soon as I'm sure I've ditched them."

Not giving his friends any time to rebuff his plan, Hesch counted to three and then pushed them toward the exit. Once in the hall, they could hear the chaotic clomp of monitors stomping through the stairwells and headed their way. Joanna locked eyes with Hesch for a moment, snatched him up with a tight hug, then pushed him off toward the sound of incoming danger. Grabbing Chih's hand in hers, they took off through the exit.

The glow dashed ahead. Heschel's chest burned as his adrenaline began to pump. He was confident the luminous being had formulated the plan, and that for it to work he would have to give everything he had to keep in step. *One and the same - same as one,* he repeated with a wave of clarity he'd never experienced reciting the old Anti-Libertas motto. Just as the stairwell door began to open, the glow led him into a narrow, unseen coat closet in the main hall. He had barely tucked his legs into the back corner when a herd of monitors rushed past. Hesch listened as the door to the balcony opened, boots shuffled around, then closed with a distinct click. *This might work out better than I thought!*

The glow was off again, this time right through the wall. Hesch raced to keep up as it coursed down the stairs, through the long, winding, dark halls of Chagrin Center, and out through the main entrance. Hovering by the giant oak at the center of the courtyard, the sphere changed. Hesch was stunned, thinking for a moment that it took the shape of a man like a vague silhouette before darting off between the western dorms. He peered through the glass door, ensuring the path was clear before easing it open and slipping out. Once outside, with a clear route to run, he released the decoy.

"Caw, caw, ca-caw!" he crowed, using his hands like a megaphone. The sound echoed throughout the courtyard startlingly loud. "Caw, caw, ca-caw!" *Come and find me, you brainwashed badgers.*

He was just between the buildings when the sound of monitors shouting his location rang out across the compound. The edge seemed to glow in the moonlight. The last time he had run this course, the rain and the cold had nearly done him in. The last time things didn't end well.

I can do this. Lead 'em to the edge. Ditch 'em near the

falls. They'll search the woods for hours. By then, Chih will have found everything we need, I hope...and then, well, I guess I don't know what we'll do. Wait, where's the glow? Heschel was lost in his thoughts running along the edge when the light disappeared. Had he been focused, he would have followed it beneath a shrub in the shadows not far ahead. He would've executed the plan flawlessly.

"Hey, you! Observer!" The angry voice seemed to emanate from the moonlight. Heschel couldn't tell if they were ahead or behind. "I swear if you don't stop this mutiny, we'll fill your fragile frame with more voltage than vitabread in a microwave!"

Monitors positioned along the edge stepped out from every shadowy nook within a twenty-foot radius. They moved in, systematically keeping their shock rifles fixed on his torso. His cheeks flushed as his heart began to race. *It's not going to end like this. It can't. I'm not gonna fry our plan out here! Glow? What do I do?*

Fully encircled, the young WAFE took a deep breath, cupped his hands in front of him, and watched as the glow appeared before their eyes. Crackling like a Tesla coil, lightning bolts like spider legs reached out toward the monitors in terrifying flashes. *It's just you and me,* said Hesch to the glow. *One and the same - the same as one... alright? Just don't break them. We're not monsters. People over progress, alright?*

"Not again!" the lead monitor shouted. "I don't know

what it is or where I've seen it, but the last time this happened, we…we…I don't remember. Let's all calmly step back and lower our rifles. Don't set it off. Don't give it a reason to ignite."

Hesch watched as the squad slowly retreated, keeping their eyes fixed on the electrified glow in the palm of his hands. "My friends and I aren't trying to hurt anyone. As Lieutenant Kresreb said, this isn't about sides or teams. It's about truth. We're on the side of truth—that's all!"

"Your truth or The Chamber's?" replied a more understanding voice.

"There's only one, isn't there? We can't both be right. Maybe in bits and pieces, but this is truth at the core of everything we know. Everything *you* know. You were like me once. You were all Compound 40 Observers. We've all been told that there's nothing magical, mysterious, or supernatural about life…yet here we are. You can see it. You can feel it in your chest. I know you can. I know that it burns," pleaded Hesch, grabbing his chest. "It's truth, and it's burning away the lies and the deceit and the ignorance. And you remember it, don't you? From the courtyard!"

"Don't listen to them. Don't listen to anything they say!" said the deputized monitor, growing frustrated.

"Please…just take the devices from your arms and toss them on the ground along with your rifles," requested Heschel, wiping sweat from his forehead. "Do that, and the glow won't have to get physical. That's all. Please."

"Monitors…" muttered the deputy in charge. His voice wobbled, briefly unsure of his next move. "FIRE!"

The sudden burst of power raged like an electrical storm violently channeled into Heschel. Shock darts launched inward from all directions as the glow exploded outward into dozens of jagged lightning bolts. In an instant, nearly every monitor went blind and deaf. Some dropped their rifles, rubbing their eyes and clawing at their bleeding ears. Others twisted and turned in fear of another attack from the glowing enemy.

At the center of the chaos stood Hesch, eagerly waiting for the glow to finish its defense. The lead monitor was directly in front of him, within arm's reach, yet physically untouched. Slowly he unlatched his device and flung it to the mossy forest floor beside his rifle.

The glow encircled the two of them. As it did, visions of the not-too-distant past flashed like old photos in Heschel's mind.

You were there. You were the one who took me away from my family! I can see it. Do I have a sister? Is that what you're showing me? Is it true? Where did you take her? You remember, I know you do. You have to! Why aren't you saying anything?

"Because I don't remember. I don't know where these memories are coming from. We don't get to keep them.

They aren't mine to keep. The Chamber owns them. That's part of the deal. The Chamber decides which memories stay and which go," he said, his eyes staring directly into Heschel's. "It's what makes the Anti-Libertas so strong. We don't have to remember. We don't have to decide what's right or wrong. We don't have to regret."

"Regret?" Heschel repeated under his breath. He had never thought about that concept on a personal level. There had never been a need. He simply obeyed. But now, if the truth was more extensive than The Chamber, then regret must exist. Suddenly he felt a burning urge to get out of there and join his friends in the museum. His stomach twisted at the thought of another troop catching them off-guard. The glow flashed one final time, and like a magician's sleight-of-hand, it reappeared as a soft orange ball above Heschel's shoulder. The monitor, sapped of all energy, collapsed to the ground alongside his unconscious troops.

19 USB or Bust!

"How are we gonna do this?" Chih-ming asked in a hushed voice from the center of the billowing ferns beside Chagrin Center—back where they started.

"Shhh! Just listen to the glow, Ming," gruffed Joanna. "Don't you feel that compression on your chest? Like something or someone is holding you back. Keeping you from blindly walking into the bite of a shock dart."

"I don't know, you know," he stammered. "I'm still new to this whole invisible guide thing. Last time it pushed me around like I was some old analog animatronic cave dweller. Like I wasn't smart enough or strong enough to do anything myself."

"Well…would you have?" asked Joanna.

"Would I have what?"

"Would you have done it yourself? Could you have?" she gently wondered. "Would you have found our secret cubby and those clues without the glow illuminating your path while filling you with a super-dose of bravery?"

"Well…I…When you put it like that…." Chih mumbled, picking at the ferns and shuffling his feet in the soft dirt.

"I'm not tearing you down, Ming. None of us would be here if the glow hadn't pushed and pulled and protected," she said, pulling the small fern branch from him and squeezing his hand tight. He looked up in surprise. No one at Compound 40 had ever held his hand like that. "None of us. But the glow seems to know what each of us needs to move forward. To grow and listen and filter this information through our hearts and minds. You just needed a kick in the butt."

Chih-ming stared at Joanna. Remembering what Heschel had said on the balcony, he pulled his shoulders back and stood a little taller, trusting her with the next move. No matter where it led.

From around the corner, they watched as a giant, flame-like orb darted from the main entrance of Chagrin Center to the center of the courtyard near the big oak. Chih threw his hand over Joanna's mouth as she gasped at seeing the glow momentarily taking the shape of a human before heading off between the dorms. Not long after, they watched their friend exit the building and pause in the middle of the path.

"What's he doing?" whispered Joanna. "He's going to get himself arrested!"

"Shhh! Trust the plan, right?" said Chih.

They both jumped at the loud and surreal crow caws ringing out from their friend. Several resonating squawks echoed throughout the courtyard. In an instant, Heschel was off chasing the glow, followed by the crashing sound of the main doors bursting open, voices shouting, and boots stomping.

"It's time," Joanna whispered, taking off toward the main entrance.

The courtyard was silent except for a few crows now cawing high up in the oak tree. The hallways were uncomfortably quiet too. So was the museum. The lights were on everywhere, dim and flickering, as though the building was aware of the chaos unfolding and wanted to hide.

Chih didn't waste a second firing-up the computer he had spent so many hours at nearly every night for years.

"Hey, J, take these, would you? I need you to organize the keywords from lowest to highest," requested Chih, his voice confident and his mind clear. "We'll need them as soon as the back-end of Stream loads."

Joanna had the keywords lined up in three rows of four

and ordered according to the corresponding pew number, lowest to highest.

"Toss me the USB, would you?" he said, holding up his long arm.

"It's right…" said Joanna, trailing off and beginning to dig around her carryall frantically. "It was right here! It was inside the inner lining pocket. The pocket was unzipped. It's gone, Ming! It's gone!" Joanna pulled the carryall from her side, turning every pocket inside out. Panicking, she ripped open the seems. "I know it's here, Chih. I had one job. I know it's here!"

Chih tapped her on the shoulder and took a stab at searching through the bag. She was right. It was nowhere. Dropping onto all fours, they crawled all around and beneath the desk. Nothing. Joanna's heart was racing and her cheeks bright red when she paused to calm down. As she did, she felt a small, solid, rectangular object beneath the cloth of her jumpsuit.

"It's the USB!" she shouted, hunkering down and covering her mouth as soon as she said it. "I forgot I moved it to my shoulder pocket when we were hiding in the ferns. I thought the carryall might be a little too obvious."

Dizzy from the rush, Chih took hold of the drive and carefully plugged it into an open port. A small window popped on the screen that read Reset your wallet by entering the keyphrase.

"Reset?" echoed Joanna. "Does this mean the file's gone? We don't want to reset it. We just want access, don't we?"

"No. I mean, yes. I mean, we're good, Joanna," said Chih, stammering his way into clarity. "This is how they protect their data. Whoever they are. We just need the words to unlock it, reset the connection, then slip into their ledger. It's wild, though. That someone on the outside, a Deplorable, would have access to ancient words hidden for years on C-40 pews and connected to a stone tablet buried beneath a waterfall. It's super strange, don't you think?"

"Ming, to be honest, I don't have enough room in my head to think about how this is happening. Okay?" said Joanna, taking a deep breath before firmly and ferociously saying, "Let's do this."

"Feed me!"

"Here goes...wait...I forgot the numbers don't mean anything! And the words are all in Greek! I can't read them, Ming," she said, frustration building again.

"You know what, hand 'em over. It'll be easier for me to translate anyhow," said Chih, his eyes beginning to glow as he grabbed hold of the first one.

Joanna shook her head in surprise with puffed cheeks and a mighty exhale. "Whoa! That's still just as weird as it was the first time. Not sure I'll get used to seeing those eyes glow."

She handed them over, one paper note at a time in ascending pew order. With each initial glance at the Greek symbols, Chih-ming's eyes flashed brighter. He would read the note, then close his eyes tight, picturing each word in it's proper place on the tablet while shaking his head, imaginatively flipping through a visual catalog of Greek to English translations. Joanna would hand him a paper and look away until he asked for another, unsettled by the fleshy pink glow of his eyelids.

"That's it!" he shouted. "I had to retranslate a couple of words. You know, different languages carry multiple meanings for similar words, but I got it. We got it!"

"So we're in?" Joanna asked.

"Wait, wait, wait, wait, wait…What's this? An eight-digit pin?" Chih threw his hands in the air. His long arms hung over his head in frustration. "I can't believe it! I can't believe I never thought of additional security. It's like amateur hour all of a sudden!"

"Extra security? You mean we can't get in with the key?" Joanna whispered, the burning in her chest rising in force. "We've got to be able to access it. I feel it, Chih. Repeat it. Repeat the phrase. There's gotta be another clue in there. How about the pew numbers?"

"Nope. Too many. We need eight, not twelve," he mumbled, bobbing his head and thinking through options. "Okay, okay. Here goes…'If you love me you will do what

I command. I will ask the father and he will send you another helper to be with you forever, the spirit of truth who the world cannot accept'…anything?"

"Chih, do you think that *helper*, that *spirit of truth*, might be the glow?" asked Joanna, watching the glow over Chih's shoulder flare and flicker as he recited the secret passage.

"Numbers, Joanna. Not philosophical musings," Chih replied.

"We need to ask the glow. We need its help, Ming. I can't believe I didn't catch it before. It's the helper, of course it is! The orb is that…that spirit," Joanna stammered, her red hair disheveled and covering her eyes. It was the first time Chih took notice of the freckles on her flushed cheeks. In fact, he hadn't noticed individual quirks and traits before the orb rocked his world. Quiet as a librarian, Joanna held her hands palms up the way Heschel had done in the courtyard weeks before. *Glow, I don't know how this works. I just believe that you're here to help and that you're pushing for the truth.*

Chih-ming, holding his breath, listened intently while his friend pleaded with the orb.

One more time, Ming. Recite the whole thing one more time—something's missing. Try to picture the tablets. Imagine the symbols, the words, and the placement of every line and dot.

Chih closed his eyes and began imagining the tablet

pieces. Starting with the title, he began to recite it from top to bottom. "John fourteen, fifteen through seventeen, 'If you love me you will....'"

"Wait!" Joanna shouted. "That's it!"

"The reference numbers? Doh! So obvious...14151617. John, whoever you are, you're a genius!" said Chih, his head bobbing and hips swaying as he typed. "We're in!"

"Look at that! Millions of Libertas Tokens. And check out all those transactions, Ming. Thousands! It looks like some were even made today," she pointed out, her voice dropping to a whisper as she spoke. "How on the edge are we gonna find this thing when we're not even sure what the thing is?"

"I think I know," said Heschel, gasping for air and leaning on the doorframe.

20 The Stone's Edge

"Heschel had run straight to the museum. He ran faster through the woods and across the compound than he ever thought necessary. Maybe it was the glow or the gut feeling that lives were at stake. Whatever it was, he tore across the grounds like a phantom's shadow, weaving in between gaggles of monitors without so much as a glance in his direction.

"I was hoping...you two...wouldn't have finished... the job without me," said Hesch, shoulder's heaving as he made his way towards his too-shocked-to-move partners. With each weary step, the orbs over their shoulders seemed to glow brighter.

"I didn't think I'd actually see you again," whispered Joanna, reaching out to help Hesch drop into a seat by the desk. "I thought...I guess I thought you'd, you know...do what Charlie did."

"Die?" said Chih-ming, surprised by Joanna's dark greeting. "A little doom and gloom, don't you think, Joanna?"

"Sacrifice," Heschel replied. "He didn't *just* die...if he is dead. He sacrificed himself for our escape with this...." Pulling out the tablet halves still caked with mud and clay along the edges, Hesch handed each of them one to review.

Chih's eyes lit up with an incredible glow like headlights on an abandoned country road. Snatching the other half from Joanna's hand, he held them together, rotating them sideways and staring intently through the mud.

"It's not the dry clay I care about," he mumbled. "It's what's beneath it. Here, Hesch, spit on this, would you?"

The exhausted WAFE choked, hocked, and spit on the stone without hesitation. *I haven't come this far to second guess the weird intentions of a guy with glowing eyes.*

"You do that half, and I'll take care of this one," said Chih, spitting and scraping and wiping the onyx clean. "Numbers and letters...*Hack!*...in English...*Snort!*... completely surrounding the plaque."

Joanna's red cheeks turned pale. She stepped away as her stomach twisted and turned with every coughing hack and juicy hock. After several long minutes, she shouted, "For the love of the edge! I think I'm witnessing a new level of masculine grossness. Could we please try something else?"

"There! All set," said Chih-ming, placing his tablet on the desk. Heschel followed suit. The tablet, now pieced together, looked brand new. "Joanna, you read. I'll type. This is it. We're so close!"

"I'm not touching those!" she shot back. "I wouldn't push them into a fire with a twenty-foot pole while wearing a hazmat suit soaked in antibacterial goop."

"She has a point," said Hesch. "It's fifty percent my saliva. I should read it. So where do I start?"

"Oh…Ummm…I guess just look for the numeral one if it's on there."

"Guys?" said Joanna, now staring at the museum entrance. "Guys, are your chests burning again? I think I hear something echoing through the halls. Steps maybe."

"Yeah, I feel it," said Chih.

"Me too," said Hesch, searching the stone for a 1. "I think it means we're getting close!"

"I think it means they're getting close! Listen." Joanna jogged over to the door and pulled it shut. The magnetic locks had been disabled, which meant anyone could enter at any moment. While the others began to punch random sequences into the search bar, she scanned the room for anything that might cinch the door shut from within.

Across the library, lying on the desk next to Hesch, she saw the remains of her satchel in the light of the orb.

"My carryall. MY CARRYALL! Twine. Hesch. FEET! You! On the floor by your feet!" she yelled like a crazy-person shouting out a word-salad. Without skipping a beat, Heschel snatched up the spool and tossed it across the room toward the glowing orb and directly into her sweaty palms. As quick as her tired hands allowed, she wove the string between the door handle and a steel rail bolted to the wall beneath the window. Over and under until the spool ran out. *That'll give us a few minutes…I hope.*

"Hesch, we're in!" said Chih, his voice trailing off in thought as he clicked on the exact transaction link they had finally confirmed.

"I don't get it, Chih," said Heschel. "It's a financial transaction. It's nothing but a digital logbook of deposits and expenditures. What do you think the Deplorable wants us to find?"

"Transactions hold more than just technical data, Hesch," said Chih. His voice was soft and calculated, like a session leader choosing their words carefully to draw attention to their point. "Think about an email with an attachment. The attachment is the goal of the email. It's the core value, the reason the email is sent. And the message you type within the email is simply an added note clarifying the attachment. Transactions hold notes. We don't care about the tokens. We want the note."

"So we're looking for a note within the transaction?" Hesch clarified. "How do you know that, Ming? That wasn't covered in any Seeker session. What if it's a trap?"

"I hate to break up this lesson on blockchain tokenomics, but it's now or never, you two," said Joanna. She had just pulled a chair up to the desk when they heard the command from the other side of the door.

 # 21 Off the Chain

"**I**'m counting to five," growled a snarky monitor fortified on the other side of the crudely secured door. "We all know what happens if you don't obey," he warned, slowly raising his arms as if to display the armed squad filling the hall. The monitors, however threatening they looked, were equally uneasy at the sight of blazing orbs hovering above the students.

It was a fair warning, too—of course they knew what would happen. They had managed to overcome every ounce of wretched re-education. They had been threatened, hunted, shot at, and only one option remained.

"His voice is familiar, don't you think?" said Hesch,

hunched over and squinting as though listening through another catalog of sounds. He seemed oblivious to the rather important warning the familiar voice had uttered. "It can't be!"

"Hesch, are you hearing what I'm hearing? It doesn't matter what the monitor sounds like, does it? They want us out of the picture. They want us gone. They want us dead!" said Joanna, her heart beating faster and faster with every word.

"It's the Deplorable, Joanna." Hesch straightened his back, lifted his head, and stared her straight in the eyes. "It was a set-up. Just think about it. The man in the cafeteria knew our names. He knew what we looked like. He knew where to find us. He cleared the cafeteria for us. He knew we'd trust him. So did Chicanery."

"But the glow that day…in the cafeteria…it was real," said Joanna, her cheeks flushed and her voice trembling.

"The glow wasn't approving the Deplorable. No...No...It was cautioning us to beware!" he mumbled, trying to make sense of the twisted possibility."

"How's this even possible? And what was the secret meeting in Chagrin Center all about? I'm not wimping out or anything, Hesch, I just can't picture it, and I don't want to end up like Kresreb. For the first time, I'm uncontrollably horrified—more scared than I felt on the edge or in the re-education center. And I'm tired of these emotions pulling me in every direction. Aren't You? I want to find out what a family is. I want to know real history before the Alphabet Coup reimagined it. I want to find out the source of the glow. I just don't want to…."

"It's strange, isn't it?" cut in Hesch, who only seemed to grow more confident in light of the betrayal. "We can feel the glow burning in our chests. We can see it attached to our shoulders. We've experienced its power in the deepest parts of our being. I think I even saw it take the shape of a human back in the courtyard…and yet my legs still shake, and my stomach turns at the first sign of trouble. It's as if the glow, this helper, hadn't already proven itself. As if it weren't the only reason we're still here. I guess I'm saying that I want to be around long enough to figure this out too, Joanna."

"Hesch? So, you know what you were saying about a trap a minute ago?" said Chih, who had been diligently sifting through the contents of the digital wallet.

"It's a fake wallet, isn't it?"

"No, it's genuine," said Chih, startled by the shrill sound of the library door handle being mutilated by a power saw from the hall. "It's just that, well, the USB was bugged. When we unlocked it, we sort of unleashed a whole host of viral bots directly into the account. Look, the tokens are being withdrawn from the wallet in batches by the thousands. Read the note attached to each new transaction."

Progress before people. Progress before people. Progress before people. Hesch read. "Chicanery! We've been fooled into helping The Chamber. But what about the note?"

"The note the Deplorable wanted us to find?" asked Chih. "Wouldn't that be fake too?"

"That transaction number was carved in stone. No way that's been faked," said Hesch. "They want the note, but they couldn't get to it. We had the key and the transaction number...and now they're after it all."

Chih, clicking through several tabs and mumbling under his breath, was about to read the note attached to the secret transaction when the screen went blank. The power to the museum had been cut. Now the only objects with any electrical current were the orbs still hovering over their shoulders, casting a soft yet eerie candlelit glow across each of their surprised faces.

"Listen up, fugitives. So far, I've been gracious, wouldn't you agree?" said the lead monitor from the hall, sounding a little too happy. Cutting through the door had failed. The hall was silent, and the monitors that had filled the hall were nowhere to be seen. "What can I say? I'm a patient individual who desires to see every student at C-40 identify as a victor. However, it seems to me you've chosen a rather deplorable path. You're traitors. I don't care for traitors. Now time's up."

With that final word of warning, he smiled, turned from

the entryway, then calmly walked down the dark hall and out of sight. "FIVE!" he shouted from a distance.

The explosion sent dangerous shards of door and frame soaring through the museum, leaving a gaping, crumbling hole in the wall. The students, nearly sliced to pieces, were saved by a wave of fire and smoke that knocked them onto their backs. A little dizzy and a bit unstable, all three clawed for one another in confusion. The orbs had vanished, and the only light came from several monitor flashlights waving back and forth, scanning the room through the haze.

"Hesch…I'm done," Joanna coughed. "We're just students."

"It's over, man," Chih-ming shouted over the ringing in his ears. "They won!"

The WAFE Observer sat up, watching the light flash back and forth through the smoke. The scene was chaotic as the fire alarm rang loud and monitors' shouted commands. Sitting between his friends, he gently placed a hand on each of them. The comfort of physical touch was no longer awkward. Somewhere between his mind and his gut, the glow stitched together what The Chamber had severed. He caught on that a pat on the shoulder or a hug from a friend calmed fear, tempered anger, and built stronger bonds than the Anti-Libertas could ever manufacture on Stream. That friendly touch had become the difference between giving up and getting up.

"It's the only way in or out, but you already know that don't you, Heschel of the Bantu peoples of Somalia," declared the familiar voice belly laughing from behind the dark wall of smoke.

Hesch's eyes lit up as he flashed a glance toward Joanna. The burning in his chest flared, and he jumped to his feet. *Somalia? Bantu people? My family?*

"Deplorables as far as the eye could see," the monitor grumbled. "Bodies packed around the plane begging us to take their kids—to train them in the Anti-Libertas way. Selfish people…clamoring for food, water, and medicine. Like all the rest across the globe—they didn't want our system, just our supplies. I would have been in and out of that country with half a dozen prospects in minutes. But no! Chicanery always has to have it his way. You people of the light…sheesh! I'll admit there's something different about you, but no matter how much Anti-Libertas we bake into your brains…you always go astray. Every compound, same story."

"Why do you do it? If everything fails, why do you keep forcing it? Look at you! You're twisted up in half-truths and callous to all this violence," thundered Hesch. "You chant unity but tear apart families and dissect students from reality. You're a liar! A puppet! And that show you put on in the cafeteria to trick us...well...."

"Whoa now!" said the monitor, his jolly voice replying from the smoky haze just beyond Heschel's reach. "I might be a liar now and again, or even a puppet for the good of C-40, but an actor? Nope. Never been one to sneak around like a snake undercover."

"Why would I trust you to tell the truth? You just admitted that you'd lie for The Chamber," Hesch argued.

"You're not the brightest star in the sky," said the monitor with a smirk. "I'll let you in on a little secret since you've proven pretty good at keeping a few. That little security disaster from the cafeteria is what they call my twin sibling. My flatmate before The Chamber outlawed twins for obvious reasons."

"So you know your family? Your brother? And you chose The Chamber instead?" said Hesch, sweat rolling down his face. "So the cafeteria wasn't a trap after all?"

"No and yes," said the monitor, looking at his device and straightening his suit. "No, my twin abandoned The Chamber. And yes, it was still a trap. We have eyes and ears all over the countryside—a few tokens for a few tips. We didn't have to touch the USB. He gave it to you, and the system behind Stream recognized it as a foreign device. Once you entered the keyphrase, our bots entered the wallet. They're probably hard at work right this very minute! My share of the tokens may just be the largest yet, all thanks to you. Alright, troop. Light them up!"

From all directions, shock darts whipped through the air, their electrified tips leaving streamers of light in their wake from one end of the room to the other. Chih-ming and Joanna huddled together on the floor unharmed. Hesch, on the other hand, absorbed each round as though he were a magnet purposefully drawing every dart toward its intended target—himself. Only a few seconds into the barrage, he collapsed to the ground. His body twitched violently as his eyes rolled backward. Electrical currents bounced from each dart protruding from his body, designed to keep the pain flowing.

The firing stopped.

"Sometimes, Heschel, it's simply easier to dispose of the problem than try and solve it," said the deputized monitor stepping out of the dark and into the beam of a flashlight pointed at the young WAFE's body.

The troop of monitors, stepping out from the haze, began to encircle the students, each shining a light on their motionless bodies at the center. The lead monitor, chuckling, nudged Heschel's foot with his own, the way you might check a deer hit by a truck on the highway.

"Don't you kick him like that!" Joanna shouted, throwing herself over Heschel's body. She could feel the bite of each electrical jolt as they danced between the darts.

Chih sat up in a panic clenching his teeth. Though ready to give up only a minute ago, he squeezed his fists tight in defense.

With a guttural sound that utterly terrified everyone in

earshot, Heschel opened his mouth wide and began to shout what sounded like some ancient, otherworldly, tribal war cry. Over and over, he called. Louder with every new breath. "Hoo-hah!" Deep breath. "Hoo-hah, ru-ahh!"

"This one's got a little more fight left in them!" shouted the lead monitor as the surrounding monitors clipped fresh shock darts into empty cartridges. "Troops…turn up the heat!"

Don't be scared, you two. The glow is shielding me. And the tablet is right. The Chamber can't accept him. But that lying monster of a monitor is right too—once in a while, a sacrifice has to be made for the good of the whole. I understand it now. I think you do too. As Heschel comforted his friends internally, his physical body continued chanting. At the same time, another barrage of darts shredded his drab gray uniform, embedding their claws into his swollen and bloodied skin. *Chih, you were able to screenshot the hidden message before we lost power, right? Get Joanna to safety along the edge by the falls, then read it together. Joanna, you'll know what to do after that. I believe in you. Believe in the glow. A murder, right?*

Darts continued to rain down when the unimaginable happened. Chih and Joanna, sensing the glow about to work, opened their eyes to see Heschel's body slowly rise from the floor. With his head back and his arms limp, the young student hovered nearly three feet from the ground as though floating on an invisible body of water.

"Hoo-hah! Hoo-hah, ru-ahh!" continued Hesch with a deep voice mysteriously still full of strength.

Of all the wild events Joanna had witnessed, the sight of her friend floating in the air rattled her to the core. She watched in amazement as light began to well up within Heschel. In the same way a thumb glows when pressed over a flashlight, Hesch's body began to glow a brownish, fleshy hue. As if filled to the brim and with nowhere to go, light erupted from the shock dart pin holes littering his body. Darts clinging to his skin shot out in reverse like corks from champagne bottles. Beams of light burst from his fingertips and the soles of his feet. Joanna squealed when the light flared from his eyes, ears, and mouth. It was as if his entire body had been pressurized with a sunrise and finally found release, spraying light across the room in disorienting waves.

The helper will guide you. Prepare to run, said Heschel, as his body rotated upright in the air before planting his feet firmly on the floor. Directly in front of him an orb began to morph, only this time it didn't merely expand or multiply, but it stretched, reached, and flared outward in all directions. It struggled and flickered until the phantom orb finally solidified into a humanoid figure now standing face to face with Heschel.

Chih, you're ready. Take Joanna's hand. Don't stop until you hit the falls.

As the glowing figure materialized, monitors dropped

to their hands and knees, blind and terrified. Without hesitation, Chih firmly grabbed Joanna's arm, pulled her to her feet, took her hand, then ran as fast as her legs would allow.

Heschel, stunned at what he was seeing, reached out and seized the shoulder of the glowing figure.

It's time for you to carry the torch, Heschel. You're different. Set apart for something greater. No one will understand...not fully. You're a messenger like your ancestors before you—ancestors across time and tribes. Carry the torch.

With a jolt that shook Heschel to the core, the humanoid glow collapsed into a familiar orb before disappearing in a flash of light. The monitors, dizzy and weak, rose from their stupor. Stumbling around in confusion, tripping and bumping into one another, they gathered their strewn-about gear. Unable to remember the final moments, the lead monitor ordered Heschel to be cuffed, blindfolded, and gagged, then immediately transported to the hot spot. Heschel, knowing his friends were safe, submitted without a fight.

 Epilogue: 41.286515, -81.566554

"We aren't leaving 'til he gets here, Ming," she said, staring into the forest. They were standing on the same stone ledge beside the falls she had perched that night during the Sojourn.

Chih rubbed goosebumpms on his arms as his mind raced. He wanted to obey Heschel's command. After all, the glow had given his friend profound insight into the future, or at least the events happening that very night. But he also felt sorry for Joanna. She was brave and smart, but she was also scared. Scared of making the wrong decision. Afraid of how powerful the glow truly was. Terrified of losing her friend.

"Let's start with the message, Joanna," said Chih, trying to take her mind off the chaos they had just escaped. "Listen, I have it right here. I was able to snap a screenshot of it and drop it on my chain before the power went out. Good thinking, right?"

"I'm not in the mood to joke around, Ming," Joanna whispered, scanning the treeline for any sign of Hesch.

"I know, but here's the deal…Heschel said you'd know what to do once we've read it. So I need you to focus. Hesch needs you to focus. He sacrificed himself to get us here, didn't he? And he chose you to decide what happens next. That means it's important. Life or death important, ya know?" Chih took a deep breath, touched Joanna's shoulder, then opened an image on the device still attached to his wrist.

Joanna turned around, nodded, then, with cheeks glowing red under the moonlight and tears welling up, she leaned in to read the message they'd been chasing for months. After scanning the text, she paused. Stepping back with a confused look, she said, "That's not a message, Chih. What am I supposed to do with that? How can I decide what happens next when there's no note? No direction!"

"I was confused too when I first got a look at it," he said, standing a little taller. "But I get it now. Just think about your training. Where have you seen numbers like that?"

"You're right," she said, taking a deep breath.

"Orienteering. How could I forget?"

"Think about where it might lead? The people we might find when we get there. The message *is* the adventure! It *is* the answer!" said Chih, smiling wide. "Even if Hesch didn't know, the glow did. It sent us. You know what you have to do."

"We have no idea if we can trust those coordinates. Everything around here is a brainwashed, Chamber-mangled, socially-manipulated trap," she growled, her voice echoing off the valley floor and throughout the forest below. "Besides, even if it's legitimate, I'm not leaving until he shows up. He'd do the same for us."

"41.286515, -81.566554," said Chih, reciting the coordinates for both of them to hear. "He said read it together. I'm reading it together. Maybe it's a trigger for the glow to come and help, or a Deplorable to pop out of the waterfall and guide us to safety, or a bird to swoop down and whisk us off to a secret lair! At this point, not much could surprise me."

"Besides, we…we…we don't have access to maps beyond the compound. We never have, remember?" Joanna declared, trying hard to hold back tears.

"You're right. My bad. I totally forgot we don't have access to real-time satellite imaging," he said sarcastically. Joanna looked back with one eyebrow lifted. "You would be right if I were still using the Anti-Libertas approved chip in my device. But I'm not. Sooo…."

Both eyebrows' raised in shock. Immediately curiosity overcame fear and she quickly shuffled toward him. Grabbing his wrist, Joanna pulled the device towards her. "Let me see that. How far is it? Is there a town?"

"There's a town right there. Right in the center of the forest and nearly surrounded by a bending river. The river attached to these falls," he said, hinting at the mode of transportation they would have to take to get there quickly and quietly. "Looks like it would be about an hour downstream. And it's cold. Super cold. But I snagged these matches from the library floor. They're waterproof. Chamber approved."

Joanna smiled. "Okay. Okay. I get what you're doing here."

"It's been twenty minutes," said Chih. "Let's be honest, with the show he put on back there, if he were going to make it out, he'd be here by now."

"You sound as careless as a monitor! Are you saying he's…he's dead?" she said, choking on the words.

"No. Don't you feel it? He's still alive! He's doing what he said he would, sacrificing himself for the rest of us. He's staying behind so that we can go ahead. He's giving in to them so we can get up and go!" Chih stepped in her direction, towering over her. "It's time."

Joanna squinted, her cheeks pinched and her head

shaking. She turned back toward the forest and said, "It doesn't feel right. Just a few more minutes."

Chih nodded.

The moon was fading and the temperature dropping as dawn grew near. The air beside the falls and along the edge was much colder than they were prepared for. Chih watched his breath swirl and dissipate in the early light. *A few more minutes. She'll make the right choice. I know she will. She knows we need to act before it gets too light out. Before a patrol spots us. She'll do it,* he told himself.

"Come stand by me, would you?" asked Chih. "It's cold, but if we stand shoulder to shoulder, we can share some body heat while we wait. I can block the breeze."

Joanna nodded, slowly stepping backward until she bumped into him. They stood in silence watching the forest for movement, only slightly warmer.

Turning toward Joanna with a sad, yet confident, expression, he whispered, "I'm sorry. I really do trust you… but it's time." Without warning, Chih scooped Joanna up in his arms like a man carrying a bride on their wedding day. Before the sun crested the hill, and before she could resist, Chih leapt from the stone perch over the edge and into the raging springtime waterfall.

Return of the Guide Series

The EDGE: Book One

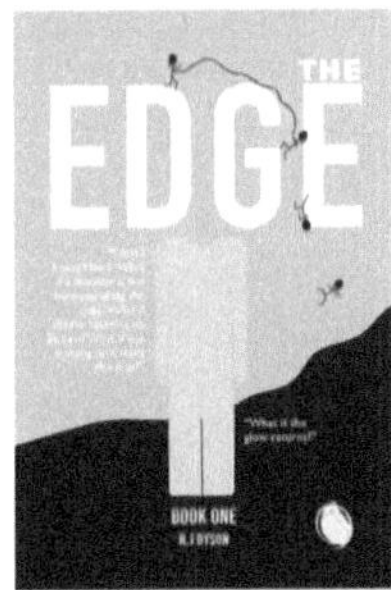

Book One Missing Chapter:
Principal Chicanery Panics

(Follow the QR Code below to download.)